The trouble didn't start till her birthday party, when Bella had emerged like a butterfly from a cocoon, blowing him away with her grace, her grown-up beauty and her devastating sex appeal.

Sergio hadn't been back to Sydney for several months, university life—and the sophistication of Rome—having more appeal than staying in a house run by a woman he disliked intensely.

He had been startled when Bella had come up to him and demanded a birthday kiss.

"You'll have to do, Sergio," she'd said without a hint of flirtation. "A girl has to be kissed on her birthday, and you're the only male here, other than Papa. And he doesn't count."

Sergio hadn't been ready for the effect on him when she'd gone up on tiptoe and pressed her mouth to his. For a split second, he'd been tempted to yank her hard against him, to part her innocent lips and plunge his tongue inside. But he'd resisted the devil's urging just in time, keeping the kiss to a platonic peck, which had obviously disappointed Bella, if her pout was anything to go by.

Well, she's not an innocent now, Sergio, he reminded himself. *Time you stopped having cold showers and started having what you've always wanted.*

Which was Bella herself, in his bed and at his mercy.

Rich, Ruthless and Renowned

Billionaires secure their brides!

International tycoons Sergio, Alex and Jeremy were best friends in college. Bonded by their shared passion for business—and bedding beautiful women—they formed The Bachelor's Club, which had only two goals:

1. Live life to the full.

2. Become billionaires in their own right!

But now, with the dotted line signed on the sale of their multibillion-dollar wine empire, there's one final thing left for each of the bachelors to accomplish—securing a bride!

The trilogy begins with Sergio's story in

The Italian's Ruthless Seduction

And look out for Alex's and Jeremy's stories, coming soon!

Miranda Lee

THE ITALIAN'S RUTHLESS
SEDUCTION

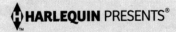

Recycling programs
for this product may
not exist in your area.

ISBN-13: 978-0-373-13415-1

The Italian's Ruthless Seduction

First North American Publication 2016

Copyright © 2016 by Miranda Lee

Printed in U.S.A.

Born and raised in the Australian bush, **Miranda Lee** was boarding-school educated and briefly pursued a career in classical music before moving to Sydney and embracing the world of computers. Happily married, with three daughters, she began writing when family commitments kept her at home. She likes to create stories that are believable, modern, fast-paced and sexy. Her interests include meaty sagas, doing word puzzles, gambling and going to the movies.

Books by Miranda Lee

Harlequin Presents

Taken Over by the Billionaire
A Man Without Mercy
Master of Her Virtue
Contract with Consequences
The Man Every Woman Wants
Not a Marrying Man
A Night, A Secret...A Child

Three Rich Husbands

The Billionaire's Bride of Innocence

Visit the Author Profile page
at Harlequin.com for more titles.

CHAPTER ONE

I SHOULD BE HAPPIER, Sergio thought as he snapped off the shower, stepped out onto the luxuriously soft bath mat and reached for an even more luxurious bath sheet. Today I became a billionaire. Today, my two best friends became billionaires as well. If that doesn't make me happy, then what will?

Sergio frowned as he dried himself vigorously. Why *wasn't* he happier? Why wasn't he thrilled to pieces with the four-point-six billion they'd been paid for the Wild Over Wine franchise? Why did signing that contract today leave him feeling just a little…empty?

Wise people did say it was the journey that gave the most satisfaction, not the destination, he conceded with a resigned shrug of his broad shoulders. The irrefutable fact was that the three members of the Bachelors' Club had now reached their destination. Well…almost. None of them had turned thirty-five yet, though they would soon. His own thirty-fifth birthday was just over a fortnight away.

Sergio smiled a wry smile as he recalled the night they'd formed the Bachelors' Club. How young they were at the time. Not that any of them had realised it back then. They'd felt incredibly mature, older at twenty-three than a lot of the other students at Oxford in their year. More confident than most as well, each of them having been blessed with good looks as well as above-average intelligence. They'd also been very ambitious.

At least, he and Alex had been ambitious. Jeremy—

who'd already had a private income—had just gone along for the ride.

It had been a Friday night, several months after they'd first met. They'd been in Jeremy's room, of course. His room had been so much bigger and better than the one Sergio and Alex had shared. They had all been more than a little intoxicated when Sergio—who had a tendency to become philosophical when he drank—had asked the others what their goals were in life.

'Definitely not marriage,' had been Jeremy's rather scathing remark.

Jeremy Barker-Whittle, youngest son of a British banking empire that went back generations. Perhaps because of their excessive wealth, his family was littered with divorce. It had not escaped his two friends that Jeremy was somewhat cynical when it came to the institution of marriage.

'I'm not interested in marriage either,' Alex Katona, a Rhodes Scholar from Sydney with a working-class background and a near-genius IQ had agreed. 'I'll be too busy working to get married. I aim to be a billionaire by the time I'm thirty-five.'

'Me too,' Sergio had concurred. Although Sergio was the only son and heir to the Morelli Manufacturing Company, based in Milan, he was well aware that the family firm was not doing as well as it once had. By the time Sergio inherited the business, he suspected it might not be worth inheriting. If he wanted to be a success in life, he had to make it on his own. Which meant no marriage as well. Not for ages, anyway.

And so the Bachelors' Club had been born, their rules and goals laid out that night with great enthusiasm.

Rule One had been somewhat sentimental—and optimistic—for three young men in their early twenties. *To remain friends for ever.*

Of course they had been very drunk at the time, having consumed quite a few bottles of Jeremy's seemingly limitless supply of fabulous French wine.

But, rather amazingly, they were still the best of friends over a decade later, despite going into business together, which would usually spell the kiss of death where friendships were concerned. Sergio didn't question why their friendship worked, but he was grateful for it. He couldn't imagine anything ever happening to spoil the bond between them.

Sergio had to laugh over Rule Two, however, which was *To live life to the full.*

Translate that to mean they were to sleep with every attractive girl who looked sideways at them. Which the three of them had managed very well during their years at Oxford. Since their graduation to real life, however, they'd become a little more discerning. At least, Sergio had, preferring the company of women who had more to offer than just their willing bodies. Women with careers and class and conversation. Often older women, unlike Alex, whose girlfriends seemed to get younger as he got older.

'Younger women don't cling or criticise or complain as much as females of my own age,' he told Sergio one day. 'Neither do they always want me to marry them.'

Alex was still anti-marriage. Not in principle. Just for himself. Unlike Jeremy, he wasn't cynical about the institution, Alex's parents and siblings having enjoyed happy marriages. As for Jeremy…he'd become a playboy of the first order, his girlfriends coming and going with alarming speed. No one could get bored with a girlfriend quicker than Jeremy. But there was always another one eager to take the previous one's place, Jeremy's wealth, good looks and charm had women falling at his feet wherever he went. Naturally, they all fell in love with him as well, a sentiment that was never returned. Jeremy wasn't into love, leaving a trail of broken hearts all over Britain, and half of Europe as well. Sergio didn't approve—and said so—but Jeremy just shrugged and said it wasn't his fault that he was fickle. It was a genetic flaw. His father was on his third marriage and his mother her fourth. Or was it her fifth?

So of course neither Alex nor Jeremy had trouble with rule number three.

Members of the Bachelors' Club must not marry till at least thirty-five.

Which had seemed an eternity away at the time.

Still, Sergio had always known, despite a huge dose of bitterness over his father's second marriage and subsequent divorce, that one day he would marry. He was Italian, after all. Family was important to him. But he'd put the idea on hold whilst he'd worked obsessively towards the Bachelors' Club's main goal.

To become billionaires by the age of thirty-five.

Which they'd finally managed. Today.

Another wave of melancholy washed through Sergio as he accepted that today also marked the virtual end of their club. Yes, the three of them would still remain friends for ever—that was a given—but only at a distance. He himself was returning to Milan shortly to take control of the family business which had gone into serious decline since his father's death last year. Alex was off back to Australia tomorrow to expand his already successful property development company whilst Jeremy would stay in London where he planned to buy himself a business. Possibly advertising. Anything but banking, apparently.

Sergio knew that once he told Jeremy and Alex tonight about his intention to marry, they would also see that the Bachelors' Club's days were seriously numbered. Still, that was life, wasn't it? Nothing stayed the same. Change was inevitable.

I will think of marriage as a new goal, Sergio decided

with determined positivity as he strode from the bathroom. A new challenge. A new journey.

So what kind of wife do you want, Sergio? he asked himself as he made his way into his huge dressing room, which housed a wardrobe that even Jeremy envied. Sergio bypassed the rack of superb Italian business suits he owned—tonight was for celebrating, not business—selecting a casually tailored pair of black trousers, drawing them on and zipping them up in a rather reckless fashion for a man of his impressive dimensions.

She would have to be reasonably young, he supposed, since he wanted to have more than one child. Certainly no older than mid twenties. She would also have to be physically attractive, he decided pragmatically, taking a white silk shirt off its hanger and putting it on. Sergio couldn't see himself marrying a plain Jane. Not stunning looking, though. Stunningly beautifully women caused a man trouble.

Sergio was buttoning up his shirt when his personal cell phone rang. He frowned as he strode back into the bedroom and over to where he'd left the phone by the bed. Only a small number of people had that particular number. Alex and Jeremy, of course. And Cynthia. He changed the number every year, liking the privacy this afforded him. No doubt it was either Alex or Jeremy, telling him they were running late. As usual. It wouldn't be Cynthia. He'd broken up with her over a month ago, and she'd long given up on a reconciliation.

Sergio's eyebrows lifted when he swept up the phone and saw that the caller ID was blocked, his lips pursing angrily at the very real possibility that some scam artist had hacked into his private number. It had happened once or twice before.

'Who is this?' he snapped down the line.

There was a short silence at the other end before a woman's voice hesitantly said, 'It...it's Bella...'

Shock slammed into Sergio with all the force of a physical blow, taking his breath away, not to mention his voice.

'Sergio?' she went on after a few seconds of strained silence. 'That is you, isn't it?'

'Yes, Bella, it's me,' he managed to say at last, marvelling at how normal he sounded. Because there was nothing even remotely normal going on inside him. His heart was pounding behind his ribs and his head...his head had ceased to process logical thoughts. For this was Bella calling him. The stunningly beautiful Bella...his one-time stepsister and long-time tormentor.

'You said...that if I ever needed your help...that I could call you. You...you gave me your number. At your father's funeral...don't you remember?' she finished on a somewhat breathless note.

'Yes, I remember,' he admitted once his addled brain plugged into his memory bank.

'I'm going to have to ring you back,' she suddenly blurted out, then hung up.

Sergio swore, then stared down at the dead phone, gripping it tightly as he struggled to resist the urge to throw the damned thing at the wall.

For a full five minutes he paced the room, willing her to call him back, wondering and worrying about what kind of trouble she was in. Not that he should care. She obviously hadn't given him a second thought since their parents' divorce. And that had been eleven years ago! Her showing up at his father's funeral last year had been all about his father, not him personally. It infuriated Sergio that he was wasting time waiting for her to call him back when he should be getting himself down to the restaurant for dinner. His booking was for eight and it was close to that now.

If he had any sense he would stop thinking about Bella and do just that.

He laughed at himself as he collected his shoes and socks and started putting them on. For when had he ever been able to stop thinking of Bella once she'd entered his head?

Maybe, if she'd remained a nobody, living a quiet life back in Australia, Sergio might have been able to forget her. But no. Fate hadn't been that kind. After winning a high-profile talent quest on Australian television shortly before Dolores asked his father for a divorce, Bella had gone on to become a famous leading lady in musical theatre, starring in shows all over the world, most on Broadway, but some of them in London. Her exquisitely beautiful face had been everywhere at one time. On television. The sides of buses. On billboards. Sergio had resisted going to see her on stage, knowing that watching her perform in person would only fuel the overwhelming desire that she'd once inspired in him, the memory of which he still struggled with.

But once again, fate hadn't been kind, Jeremy dragging him along one night about three years ago to a Royal Variety Performance where Bella—unbeknownst to Sergio—had been one of the guest performers. What agony it had been, sitting there watching her sing and dance.

But even worse had been to come that night, with Jeremy informing him after the curtain had finally gone down that he'd received an invite to the after-concert party at the Soho Hotel. Sergio could have refused to accompany him, but a perverse curiosity had overridden his first instinct, which was to go home to his new Canary Wharf apartment and get blind drunk. Instead, he'd gone to the party where Bella had waltzed in on the arm of her latest lover, a handsome French actor of dubious talent with a reputation as a womaniser. What a brilliant-looking couple they'd made, her exquisite blonde beauty the perfect foil for the Frenchman's dark good looks, Bella dressed in an ethereal white evening gown whilst he was all in black; a devil to her angel. Sergio had watched her for ages from a distance, watched her and wanted her, his jealousy fierce whenever the Frenchman had touched her. Which had been often.

Sergio no longer had a clear memory of what he'd said to her when she'd finally spotted him across the room, leaving the leech for a moment to come over and speak privately to him. He would not have been rude. That was not his way, his father having instilled politeness and manners into him from a young age. No doubt he'd said something complimentary about her performance. What he could recall, however, was the wicked cruelty of his erection as he'd watched her mouth move to say he knew not what. Never before or since had he felt anything like it, her physical closeness causing his unrequited desire for her to flare to a point almost impossible to control.

But control it, he had, conversing with her for a short while till her obsequiously possessive lover had come over and drawn her away. It was only after Sergio had arrived home and was safely alone in his bedroom that he'd given vent to his explosive emotions, smashing his fist through the bathroom door, breaking two fingers in the process, after which he'd plunged himself into a cold shower and wept like a baby.

It had taken several weeks for his hand to heal, and for him to find some perspective about his self-destructive feelings for Bella. Talking to Alex and Jeremy had helped, though their advice had been typical.

'What you need, mate,' Alex had said, 'is to get laid more often.'

'She's probably not that great in bed, anyway,' Jeremy had added. 'Alex is right. There's plenty more fish in the sea. Throw the net out a bit more, bro.'

Which he had, for a while, having sex with more women in the next month than he had for years. All of them had been one-night stands. All of them blondes with blue eyes, pretty faces and very nice figures.

In the end, however, such a lifestyle had not sat well with Sergio. So he'd found himself Cynthia, an attractive divorcee who had been very good in bed and hadn't minded that he didn't love her. Gradually, Bella had slipped to the back of his mind, where she stayed. Most of the time.

Still, when he'd heard via Alex that Bella had broken up with the French actor, Sergio hadn't been able to deny feeling some satisfaction. He hadn't felt quite so happy when he'd found out she'd taken up with a Russian oligarch who'd made billions out of oil and natural gas, investing his fortune in a string of luxury hotels. The Russian had, again according to Alex, a reputation as a notorious ladies' man with a penchant for celebrity blondes, usually supermodels or actresses. Sergio had shaken his head in dismay over this. Because it wasn't the first time Bella had taken up with a man of dubious reputation. Aside from the French actor, her list of previous lovers included a rock star with a drug problem and an Argentinian polo player who changed girlfriends as often as his horses. None of these relationships had lasted. But the gossip rags had had a field day during every one of these affairs, and afterwards.

When would Bella ever find true love? they'd speculated *ad nauseam.*

Sergio stared down at the still-silent phone, hating himself for worrying about her, *despising* himself for just wanting to hear the sound of her voice again. But why *hadn't* she rung back? She'd actually sounded nervous. And why had she hung up so abruptly? Had her latest lover come into the room and found her on the phone to another man? Was she in an abusive relationship perhaps?

Despite being successful in her career, Bella was a very bad picker of men.

Which was nobody's fault but her own!

Still…he did not like to think of her being treated badly.

Sergio swore at his tortured train of thoughts. Damn it all, she wasn't his responsibility any more. Hadn't been since the divorce. He shouldn't care about her at all! But somehow, for some perverse reason, he did care. Which was perhaps why, when she'd shown up out of the blue at his father's funeral last year, looking tired and strained, he'd given her his private phone number and told her that if she ever needed him for anything, then he would be there for her.

Perversely, he hadn't recognised her at first. She'd been wearing a large black hat, a black wig and dark glasses. Even when she'd revealed her identity to him, he hadn't reacted the way he would have expected, with a mad rush of rampant desire. When she'd expressed her condolences, then added a sincere apology for the way her mother had treated her father, his only emotion had been sadness. Looking back, Sergio could only imagine that grief over his father's death had dampened his hormones to a point where not even being in Bella's provocative presence could rouse him. He recalled actually wanting to talk to her more. But when someone else had come up to speak to him—he couldn't remember who—she'd said a hurried goodbye and disappeared.

He'd never told Jeremy or Alex that the mysterious brunette was Bella. He hadn't been into chatting, or confiding, at that particular time, depression taking hold of him for several weeks after the funeral. When he'd finally dragged himself out of the black pit, Sergio had regretted giving Bella his phone number. Not because he'd thought she would ever contact him but because his foolish gesture had brought her back into the forefront of his mind.

It had taken a supreme effort of will to push her back to a place where she was no more than a frustrating memory, but every now and then—like tonight—she would break out of the mental dungeon into which he'd locked her and give him hell.

It was pathetic, really. Exasperated with himself, he slipped his phone in his trouser pocket and headed for the door, determined not to waste another moment of headspace on that infernal woman. But within seconds of locking the door another thought crossed his mind.

Maybe she was pregnant!

This time, Sergio's laugh was both rueful and self-mocking. In the old days a single woman falling pregnant would have been a disaster. But this wasn't the old days. If Bella had happened to accidentally fall pregnant—a highly unlikely idea, he now appreciated—she wouldn't need *his* help. She had enough money to hire nannies and any other help she needed. She certainly wouldn't ask any man—especially himself—to make an honest woman out of her. That was total fantasy. As much as Sergio had had many fantasies about Bella over the years, none of them had included marriage.

Women like Bella were not made for marriage. They were made to be admired and desired. Made to be bedded, not wedded. As for children…clearly Bella had never felt the urge to reproduce. Yet she could have, if she'd wanted to. A lot of celebrity women had babies outside marriage. No, clearly Bella wasn't interested in that kind of commitment. Sergio wasn't surprised, given she'd been raised by a woman whose ambition for her daughter to become rich and famous had been nothing short of obsessive. Sergio believed Dolores had only married his father so that he could pay for her daughter's tuition in singing and dancing. She'd seduced the Italian widower when he had been lonely and vulnerable, then trapped him into marriage with a supposed pregnancy that had miraculously disappeared as soon as the ring had been on her finger. Sergio could not prove that she'd never been pregnant at all, but he'd always suspected. When she'd asked for a divorce as soon as Bella's career had taken off, his suspicions had been confirmed. Not that he'd said as much to his father. The poor man had been shattered, having truly loved Dolores. And Bella as well.

Sergio didn't blame Bella entirely for what she'd become. Stage mothers were notorious for producing damaged children. And Bella was definitely damaged. Why else would she become involved with a succession of men whose reputations preceded them and who would never make her happy? It galled Sergio that Bella lived her life like one long reality show, played out in front of the media, allowing herself to be paraded in front of the paparazzi by men who were more interested in her as a trophy than a person.

And who are you to judge, Sergio? his conscience reminded him quite savagely. She's no longer a person to you either. She hasn't been, not since the night of her sixteenth birthday party. That was the night she became your object of desire, a desire so strong that nothing, not time or distance, or having another woman in your bed, can totally obliterate it. You think you care about her? That's a laugh.

His phone ringing at that precise moment sent his heart leaping into his mouth. Snatching it out of his pocket, Sergio didn't even bother to look at the caller ID.

'Yes?' he said somewhat brusquely.

'Alex here, mate. Sorry, but we're stuck in traffic. Going to be a bit late.'

'Damn it all, Alex,' Sergio snapped, frustrated that it wasn't Bella calling him back. 'The reason I bought a place at Canary Wharf was because it was supposedly close to everything.' And also because the tower that housed his luxury apartment had a heated pool, a fantastic gym and a top-class restaurant.

'Yeah, well, Thursday night, you know. And Jeremy was pathetically slow getting dressed. Look, we shouldn't be more than fifteen minutes. Go sit at the table and have a drink till we get there. You sound like you need one.'

Sergio sighed. 'You could be right.'

'Anything wrong?'

'Not really. Just a bit tired.' He might have told them about Bella's call if he'd known what it was about. But he didn't, damn it all. Maybe he'd never know. Maybe she'd never ring back. Hell, he wasn't sure if he could stand that.

'Well, it's been a big day,' Alex said. 'But a great one. You are one incredible negotiator, buddy. Now go relax with a whisky, and we'll be there soon.'

CHAPTER TWO

BELLA DIDN'T STOP shaking for a good five minutes after she'd hung up. Even then her heart was still racing, her mouth dry, her head whirling. Never in her life had she ever had a full-blown panic attack. But she knew all about them, a colleague of hers suffering from severe panic attacks before opening nights. Bella knew all the symptoms. She'd just never experienced them personally.

Admittedly, she'd been a bit nervous before ringing Sergio, but that was only natural. She still felt guilty over the way her mother had treated his father. If she was strictly honest with herself, she didn't feel she had the right to ask Sergio for help. Not after what her mother had done. If anyone was to blame for that panic attack, it was her mother!

Bella hadn't found out till the middle of last year just how badly her mother had treated Sergio's father, Dolores admitting one night whilst supposedly giving her daughter *advice* about men and marriage that she herself had used a pretend pregnancy to trap her Italian boss into marrying her; that she'd never really loved the man; that she'd been willing to do anything to secure the financial support she'd needed to make her daughter into a star. Her earlier claim that she'd asked for a divorce because her husband no longer loved her had been a lie.

Bella had been so appalled by her mother's cold-blooded confessions that she'd felt compelled to seek out the man whom she'd once affectionately called Papa and apologise. Tracking him down had proved difficult—there was no mention of him on the internet—but she'd finally managed with the help of a private investigator, only to discover Alberto was close to death in a Milan hospital. Guilt had seen her dropping everything and flying over to Milan, determined to tell him in person that she always remembered him with great fondness and that she really appreciated all he'd done for *her*.

By the time she'd arrived at the hospital, however, he'd already died. So she'd gone to his funeral instead. In disguise, of course. She hadn't wanted to cause the family—especially Sergio—any embarrassment, knowing that if the paparazzi recognised her, then the service could turn into a three-ring circus.

It had been one of the most difficult days of her life, sitting all by herself in that huge cold cathedral, silently witnessing Sergio's palpable grief and wondering if her mother was indirectly guilty of his father's death. It was often said that stress could cause cancer. And clearly, Dolores had given Alberto Morelli loads of stress and unhappiness during the eight years their marriage had lasted.

Yet he'd never shown that unhappiness around *her*. He'd been very good to her, sweet and kind, as had Sergio, who'd been a wonderful big brother, always willing to listen to her sing, or watch her dance. Looking back, she realised he'd been amazingly patient with her, not a virtue one often associated with teenage boys. Sergio had only been fifteen when her mother had married his father, she a rather silly and very precocious ten-year-old. He'd been a quiet boy, rather reserved in personality but awfully clever. And surprisingly good at sport. They'd often played basketball together in the backyard when he'd wanted a break from his studies.

She'd missed him terribly when he'd been sent away to a university in Rome, his father not wanting him to forget his Italian roots. She'd been thirteen at the time, a very skinny thirteen, the only girl in her class not to have hit puberty. She'd only seen Sergio three times a year after that, at Easter and Christmas when he'd flown back to Sydney for a few days, then for the two weeks during July when the family had holidayed at the family villa on Lake Como.

Oh, how she'd loved those holidays! What fun the two of them had had together, swimming and boating and just generally larking around.

Not the last time, though, she recalled, Sergio spending most of his time in his room, studying for his final exams. By the following year, their parents had already separated, Sergio had gone to Oxford for further studies and she'd been on her way to Broadway, and stardom. Their relationship—which she'd imagined had been close—had suddenly no longer existed. She'd missed her big brother at first but soon she'd been consumed by her career and the attention that went with it. Out of sight had eventually been out of mind.

They'd crossed paths only once in the years since, at an after-concert party in London. She hadn't recognised him at first, he'd been so handsome and impressive looking, having finally filled out his tall, lanky frame. But his eyes had been the same. Hard to forget eyes like that. So dark and so beautiful, and she'd felt unsettled by the hardness in his gaze. It hadn't taken her long to realise he'd still been angry with her mother—and with her too, she'd supposed—his politeness having a chilly edge to it.

There'd been no chilliness in his eyes at his father's funeral, however, only sadness and a gentleness, which by then she hadn't felt she deserved. Thank God she'd been wearing dark glasses, because behind them she'd been weeping silent tears of wretchedness and remorse. She knew that she should have contacted both him and his father after the divorce. Should have shown some regret and gratitude. Some *decency*! But she'd been too caught up at the time with the sudden burst of fame, with finally being on the verge of fulfilling her mother's rabid ambition, and yes, Bella, admit it…fulfilling your own. She could excuse herself by saying she'd only been eighteen, but that was no excuse. No excuse at all!

Bella had been quite overcome when Sergio had written down his private number on a business card and told her to ring him if she ever needed anything, anything at all. His compassionate and unexpectedly generous gesture had threatened the last of her emotional control, so when a very attractive redhead had come up to them and linked arms with him, she'd stuffed the card into her handbag, said a hurried goodbye and fled before she'd burst into noisy tears in front of everyone.

Tears threatened again now. Tears of frustration and misery. She hadn't slept well last night. She hadn't slept well in ages. Truly, she could not go on like this. She had to get away. Away from everyone who she knew down deep didn't have her best interests at heart. They only wanted what they could get out of her, which was why they kept pressuring her to take on more and more work. Bella had acquired a long list of hangers-on over the last few years. At present she had a manager, a Hollywood agent, a PA, a publicist, plus her own personal stylist. Then, of course, hovering in the background, was her mother.

They all wanted their cut. All wanted their piece of her.

She had no time to herself. No time for a personal life. No time for anything but work.

Lately, she'd begun to feel as if she were on a roller-coaster ride that never stopped. *She* never stopped. Well it had to stop. *She* had to stop. And she had to stop right now!

'So stop being such a lily-livered coward and ring Sergio back,' she ordered herself.

Stiffening her spine, Bella ignored her suddenly pounding heart, grabbed her phone and hit redial.

CHAPTER THREE

SERGIO WAS SITTING at the table with the best view of the river, sipping a glass of Scotch on the rocks and doing his best to relax, when his phone rang.

His heart jumped, his gut twisting into knots as he glanced at the caller ID, a wave of relief hitting him with the force of a tsunami. Because it wasn't Alex, ringing again to say they would be even later. The caller ID was blocked. Which meant it was Bella, calling him back. Thank God. Sergio suspected he would not have been able to sleep tonight if she hadn't. He would have had to do something really ridiculous, like hire a private investigator to find out her number, or her address. Or some way of contacting her.

How pathetic was that?

Truly, Sergio, get a grip!

But it was futile advice, his fingers tightening around the phone as he lifted it to his ear. But his voice—when he spoke—sounded wonderfully calm and seemingly relaxed. 'Hello, Bella.'

'Heavens! How did you know it was me?'

'You blocked your ID,' he explained. 'No one else who uses my private number does that.'

'Oh, I see…'

'So what happened earlier? Why did you hang up?'

'Sorry about that. But Mum suddenly came to my door and I didn't want her to know I was ringing you.'

Sergio was truly taken aback. 'Your mother lives with you?'

'Lord, no. I live by myself in New York. But I came back to Sydney a few days ago for a holiday. More fool me,' she added drily. 'Look, have I called you at a bad time? Are you too busy to talk? Where are you? I can hear quite a bit of noise in the background.'

A loud group of men had just passed by Sergio's table.

'I'm in a restaurant, waiting for some friends of mine to arrive. But they're running late. London traffic is not conducive to punctuality.'

'New York's just as bad. So you're still living in London?'

'I bought an apartment here,' he told her, wondering what she was getting at. He was also beginning to see that his earlier concern for her welfare had been ridiculous. But that was typical of his reactions where Bella was concerned. They were always over the top and dangerously lacking in logic.

'So how can I help you, Bella?' he asked, knowing full well that her problem would be nothing like he'd been imagining.

'I was wondering…do you still have that villa on Lake Como? You didn't sell it after your father passed away, did you?'

'No. I would never sell the villa. It's been in the Morelli family for generations. Why?'

'I…I need to get away, Sergio. Somewhere private and peaceful. I was hoping to rent it from you for two or three weeks. Maybe even a month.'

'I see,' he said, suppressing his annoyance with difficulty. If she wanted to rent a damned villa on Lake Como there were plenty on the market. Why ask for his? One part of him wanted to tell her to go to hell. But that other part—the one that still wanted her, despite everything—could not resist the opportunity to see her again. In the flesh. Her absolutely gorgeous exquisite flesh.

'So when would you be wanting to stay there?' he asked, casually.

'Straight away,' she said. 'Or at least as soon as I can get there. Like I said, I'm in Sydney at the moment.'

At her mother's house, he thought bitterly, the one his father had generously given to that gold-digger as part of their divorce settlement.

'I gather that Dolores won't be coming with you to the villa, then?'

'Good God, no. I want to come alone.'

That shook him, since he had presumed that she would be coming with her latest lover. Suddenly, Sergio could not contain a rush of dark excitement. He'd never pursued Bella over the years, despite his obsessive desire for her. And he could have, once he was older, especially after their wine bars had been such a great success and the money had started rolling in. After all, she was no longer his stepsister, no longer forbidden fruit. So why hadn't he?

For lots of reasons, he accepted. Pride mostly. He was Italian, after all. He would not have reacted well to rejection. Running after a woman—any woman—was not his style. Running after the daughter of the gold-digger who'd broken his father's heart would have felt like the ultimate betrayal, plus the height of stupidity. After all, the apple never fell far from the tree, did it? If Bella had responded to his advances, he would never have been sure if her feelings were real, or faked, especially after he'd become seriously rich.

But this was different. Her placing herself in his debt made it different.

'I'm sorry, Bella,' he said, relishing his moment of power over her, 'but I can't let you rent the villa any time soon. I'm going to be staying there myself all during July.'

'Oh,' she said, conveying a wealth of disappointment and dismay in that one word.

'But you can stay there with me free of charge,' he offered. 'If you don't mind having a bit of company.'

'Just you?' she said, sounding slightly hesitant. 'I mean... you won't have anyone else there with you?'

'No. Just me. And Maria, during the daytime.'

'The same Maria who used to do the cooking and cleaning back in the old days?'

'The one and the same. But she doesn't live in now. She's married and lives in a nearby village with her husband, Carlo. He does the garden, when it needs to be done, and the pool, during the summer. Maria comes in regularly when someone is staying there. Which isn't all that often since my father passed away.'

Her sigh sounded sad. 'I still feel terrible about your father.'

Sergio gritted his teeth. He didn't want her apologising again.

The sight of Alex and Jeremy entering the foyer brought Sergio to a quick decision. 'I'm sorry to cut you off, Bella, but my friends have just arrived. If you could give me your phone number, I promise I'll ring you back later this evening and we'll make concrete plans.' A quick mental calculation reassured him that it would still be morning in Australia, even at midnight in London. 'Meanwhile, book a flight to Milan and get yourself packed. And for pity's sake, don't tell your mother where you're going. In fact, don't tell *anyone* where you're going. I don't want the paparazzi hovering over the villa in a helicopter trying to get a shot of the infamous Bella and her latest lover, okay?'

'What? Oh, yes, yes, I see what you mean. They do like to jump to conclusions, don't they? Especially about me. I promise I won't tell a single soul. Gosh, you've no idea how much I appreciate this, Sergio. I always—'

'Have to go now, Bella,' he interrupted brusquely. 'Your number, please?'

She gave him her number and he hung up just as Alex and Jeremy reached the table, Sergio turning his phone right off before slipping it back in his pocket.

The face he lifted to greet his friends would have looked calm enough. Sergio was not in the habit of showing his emotions, which was just as well, given the thoughts that were going on in his head. He could still hardly believe it. *Bella!* In his home and in his debt!

Sergio had never believed himself a ruthless man. Or a vengeful one. It seemed he was even more Italian than he'd thought.

'Sorry we're late,' Alex said as he pulled out a chair and sat down.

Alex, Sergio finally noted, had dressed casually in dark blue jeans and a pale blue shirt, whilst Jeremy was still wearing a suit. Not the navy pinstripe he'd worn earlier today but a superb grey three-piece with a purple shirt and a lilac tie.

'Setting up a date for tomorrow night?' Jeremy asked as he too sat down.

'Sergio doesn't go on dates,' Alex said drily. 'He has sleepovers.'

'Cheapskate,' Jeremy said, though affectionately. 'The least you can do is pay for a girl's dinner before you take her to bed. So who *are* you sleeping with these days?'

'That's none of your business,' Sergio returned coolly, deciding right then and there not to tell either of them about Bella's call. He didn't want either of his friends swaying him from the course of action he'd decided to take. 'Come on, let's hurry up and order. I'm starving.'

That was another thing about this restaurant that Sergio liked. The speed with which drinks and meals were delivered. In no time a bottle of champagne was opened and poured, two plates of herb bread arriving at the same time to soak up some of the alcohol.

It would have been a highly enjoyable evening if his mind hadn't been on other things. Namely how he was going to seduce Bella, which of course was what he had every intention of doing. In all honesty he hadn't had much practice at actual seduction. Tall, dark and handsome men—especially well-heeled ones—rarely had to resort to outright seduction. But just tall, dark and handsome might not cut it with Bella. He supposed he could tell her he was now a billionaire—women like Bella could never have enough money—but that wouldn't be nearly as satisfying as having her come to his bed willingly, not because she was attracted to his money, but because she was attracted to *him*.

Sergio mulled over what approach would appeal to Bella all through his entrée. He came to the conclusion during his main course that her relationship history suggested she was attracted to bad boys, something Sergio was not. At least…not till now.

I can do bad boy, he decided over dessert. Because of course, now that he had the opportunity, he would do anything—anything at all—to have Bella in his bed, at least once. No, not just once. *Once* would not be nearly enough to obliterate the heat that was already gathering in his tortured loins. He would need a whole month of sex before he'd grow tired of her. And not just straightforward sex either. He wanted to have her every which way there was, wanted to experience all the wildly wanton things that those other boyfriends of hers would have insisted upon.

And when the month was over, after he'd had his fill, he would send her on her merry masochistic way, after which he would set about finding himself a nice girl to marry.

Good plan, that, he decided as he devoured his last mouthful of crème caramel. Though maybe *good* was not the right word.

'You're in a strange mood tonight, Sergio,' Jeremy remarked over coffee. 'I know Alex and I are the major talkers in our trio but you usually contribute a little more to the conversation. So what gives? You having woman trouble?'

Sergio smothered a laugh. *Woman trouble* didn't even begin to describe the effect Bella's call had had on him. But he did feel somewhat calmer now that he had a definite plan in mind to deal with his ongoing and obsessive desire for her. All that remained was to execute that plan successfully and she would cease to be a problem.

Meanwhile, he decided to broach the subject he'd been going to bring up before Bella had rung. After all, the three of them might not get together again in person for ages and, as they were fellow members of the Bachelors' Club, he believed they had a right to know what his future intentions were.

'In a way,' he replied enigmatically. 'The opposite sex certainly does figure in what I am about to say.'

'That sounds ominous,' Alex said.

'Not ominous. But serious. Yes. I've decided that I'm going to get married.'

Alex sucked in sharply whereas Jeremy just smiled.

'That doesn't surprise me,' he said wryly.

'Well, it surprises me!' Alex said, scowling at Sergio. 'I thought after your father's divorce you swore off marriage for ever.'

Sergio shrugged. 'That's ancient history. Now that my father's passed away and we've sold the franchise, I feel the urge for a more settled life.' Or he would, after he'd fixed up his other, more immediate urges. 'I want a family, Alex.'

Alex sighed, then nodded. 'Fair enough.'

'So who's the lucky lady?' Jeremy asked.

'Yes, who the hell is she?' Alex joined in.

'I have no idea,' Sergio told them. 'I haven't met her yet. I was thinking of an Italian girl. Someone whose family lives in or near Milan, since that's where I'll be working from now on.'

Alex just shook his head whilst Jeremy nodded, as though in agreement. 'Good thinking, Sergio. Italian girls are passionate creatures and excellent breeders, which I presume is your main reason for getting married. To have children.'

'Yes,' he admitted. 'And I want more than one child. Which means my wife will have to be young. And pretty, of course. And preferably from a wealthy family. I'll ask the Countess to throw a few parties at her villa. She knows everyone in the district who is anyone.' The Countess was his closest neighbour at Lake Como, a wealthy widow in her fifties who'd been a good friend to his father, and him. Though naturally, he wouldn't have her arrange anything till Bella had left.

'But what about love?' Alex interjected, sounding unexpectedly horrified. 'You can't marry someone you're not madly in love with.'

'For pity's sake, Alex,' Jeremy snapped. 'Being madly in love is the worst reason to get married. Trust me. I know. My father, mother and brothers are always falling madly in love and it never lasts. Sergio's got the right idea. Marry some sweet little thing who adores you and wants nothing more than to be a wife and mother and you'll be happy as a pig in mud.' He smiled suddenly. 'You know, I always suspected you were a husband in waiting.'

'Why do you say that?'

Jeremy chuckled. 'All that righteous disapproval you exhibited when I was playing the field.'

Alex snorted. 'You're still playing the field.'

'True. It's hard to give up a game that's so much fun and which, at the risk of sounding arrogant, I have a singular talent for. Both of you have been critical at times of my callously breaking hearts but I can honestly say that not one of my ex-girlfriends think badly of me. When I break up with them I always let them down gently, and with great empathy for their feelings.'

'Oh, truly,' Alex exclaimed, but laughingly. 'What shall we do with this cockcrowing devil, Sergio? Give him a gold medal for lover of the year?'

'Possibly. His record suggests he does have great skill in that area.' A sudden thought came to Sergio. 'So how do you do it, Jeremy? I mean, say there's a girl you meet whom you fancy like mad but who doesn't fancy you back. How do you go about getting her into bed? What's your first and best seductive move? This is a hypothetical case, of course,' he quickly added. 'Maybe that's never happened to you.'

'Can't recall that it has.'

'But if it did, what would you do?' Sergio persisted.

Jeremy sipped his coffee as he gave the matter some thought.

'After today,' Alex said drily, 'he'd just have to show the girl the size of his bank balance. She'd start fancying him straight away.'

Jeremy rolled his eyes at Alex as he put down his coffee cup. 'Such cynicism. I have never had to resort to mercenary measures to get any girl I wanted.'

'Spoken by a man born with a silver spoon in his mouth,' Alex muttered under his breath.

'Boys, boys,' Sergio reprimanded. 'Behave yourselves! I am trying to do some serious research here. I want to know what tactics Jeremy would use to get such a girl interested. You too, Alex,' he suggested. 'Surely you must have come across some desirable young thing who didn't just fall into your lap. Come on, both of you. I want to know what you'd do under those circumstances.'

'Well, I suppose I would try laying on the charm first,' Jeremy said. 'Tell her how great I thought she was. Not beautiful. Beautiful women are cynical about being complimented on their beauty. Better to concentrate on their other qualities. Then if that didn't work, I would place myself in her company as much as possible but ignore her completely. Use the old reverse psychology tactic. You know the adage… *Treat 'em mean, keep 'em keen.*'

'Can't say I agree with either of those tactics,' Alex said.

'So what would *you* do, lover boy?' Jeremy asked.

'First, I would find out everything I could about her. Her background. Her friends. What she liked to do. What she *liked*. Then I would ask her out somewhere that she'd love to go, somewhere seriously special, somewhere which cost a bomb. Best seats at a concert, for instance. Or the red carpet premiere of a movie which starred an actor she liked. Then, if that didn't work, I'd say how much I admired and desired her and that if she didn't go out with me then I would have to go to Thailand and become a monk.'

Sergio could not help it. He laughed. Jeremy just looked incredulous.

'And has that ever worked?' Jeremy asked. 'The monk business?'

'Don't know. Never tried it. Never needed to go that far. Sorry, Sergio, but girls do seem to fall into my lap without much effort on my part.'

Sergio didn't doubt it. Though all three of them had been blessed in the looks department, Alex was exceptionally good-looking. Very tall and very handsome, with blond hair, blue eyes and a body that he'd honed to perfection in the gym.

'You won't have any trouble getting any girl you want,' Alex directed at Sergio. 'But don't go rushing into marriage, mate. You've waited this long. Give true love a chance.'

'I never realised you were such a romantic,' Sergio

said, suddenly anxious to get this dinner over and ring Bella back.

'Me either,' Jeremy intoned drily. 'I can see that our bachelors' club might be losing two of its members soon, not just one.'

Alex just smiled. 'Not me. I don't have any plans to settle down any time soon. If ever. I'm much too busy. I have a golf resort to finish for starters. You know the one.'

'Not sure that I do,' Sergio said.

'The one you bought after the owner went bankrupt?' Jeremy asked.

'Yep. Got a bargain, I did. But it's a massive project, one which needs me to be hands-on a good deal of the time. I've already worn out one set of tyres driving to and fro up there. At the same time, I've got a few blocks of units going up in Western Sydney. With interest rates so low, the real-estate market there is booming. Truth is if I hadn't found the most perfect little PA last year who does everything for me bar tie my shoelaces, I wouldn't even have time to have sex.'

'Hmm.' Jeremy's glance was speculative. 'Is she attractive, this perfect little PA of yours?'

'Actually yes, she's *very* attractive. I like being around attractive people. But I'm not an idiot, dear friend. Harry's very much engaged and very much in love. I never mix business with pleasure.'

'A sensible rule,' Sergio said. 'I suppose her real name's Harriet,' he added, knowing Alex's penchant for nicknames. He'd actually tried to call Jeremy Jerry when they'd first met, till Jeremy had put his foot down.

'And what about you, Jeremy?' Sergio asked. 'Anyone special in your life at the moment?'

'Can't say that there is. I do date, of course. But no one special. Trust me when I say I will be a member of the

Bachelors' Club till the day I die. Possibly the only member, by the sounds of things.'

'You don't have to marry, you know,' Alex said. 'You could always live with someone. Have a baby, even.'

'I don't like babies,' Jeremy said offhandedly. 'I also don't want to live with anyone. I like living by myself. I like being selfish.'

Alex frowned. 'You're not selfish. You're a very warm, generous man and a terrific friend.'

Jeremy came as close to blushing as Sergio had ever seen.

'And you, my friend,' Jeremy shot back whilst trying not to look too pleased, 'are the biggest bull-dust artist in the world. You could sell ice to Eskimos. You're going to make another billion before you're finished.'

'I sincerely hope so,' Alex concurred. 'I have a lot of poor people to house and their kids to educate.'

'You and your charities,' Jeremy said. 'I suppose you'll be hitting me for more donations after today.'

'Absolutely. And you too, Sergio. I'll email you both with the details and amounts. Now I don't know about you two, but I'm bushed. It's been a long day. On top of that, I have a twenty-three-hour flight back to Sydney tomorrow. So let's get the bill. Sergio, you can pay since you got the lion's share today.'

'My pleasure,' he said, and reached for his wallet.

CHAPTER FOUR

'I DON'T UNDERSTAND why you can't tell me where you're going,' Dolores complained. 'In fact I don't understand why you have to go anywhere at all! I thought you'd come home to have a holiday.'

Bella glanced up from her packing to give her mother a droll look. 'It's hardly a holiday when you keep hammering away at me to do that movie Charlie wants me to do. If I've told you once, Mum, I've told you a thousand times, I do not want to do movies.'

'Then why did you get yourself a Hollywood agent?'

'I didn't. Josh did. I only agreed because at the time some famous producer in Hollywood was thinking of making a movie version of *An Angel in New York*. I would have done that. After that project fell through I kept Charlie on because I thought maybe some other party might pick up the option. But that hasn't happened yet. Meanwhile, I do not intend to do some second-rate musical which just wants to use my name to get distribution.'

'How do you know it's second rate?'

'I've read the script. And the songs are rubbish.'

'Scripts can be changed. And songs can be rewritten. Charlie says they've hired a top director.'

Bella sighed. 'See what I mean? You just won't stop. That's why I'm going away. And why I'm not going to tell you where I'm going. It's not as though you can't still contact me on my mobile,' she added, immediately making a mental note to turn the infernal thing off the moment she hit Lake Como. 'Now would you please leave me alone? I have to finish packing and I need to leave for the airport soon.'

That was a lie. Bella hadn't even booked a taxi yet. She had, however, secured a flight to Milan, leaving Mascot later today. Not a direct flight, of course. They didn't seem to exist from Sydney. She would have to endure a couple of stops. One in Singapore and then again in Rome. It was going to take her eons to get there but, hopefully, she might get some much-needed sleep on the way. Also hopefully, Sergio wouldn't let her down when he finally rang back. If he changed his mind about her staying at his villa, then she'd go anyway and check into a hotel on Lake Como. Lots of the large old villas had been made into boutique hotels.

Bella had every confidence, however, that Sergio would not let her down, not after telling her to book a flight. Sergio had obviously matured into a decent man, like his father. Nothing like the kind of man she kept getting mixed up with and who always let her down in the end.

'It must be somewhere warm, by the look of the clothes you're taking,' her mother said, having not moved an inch from where she was standing at the foot of the bed, her arms crossed, her expression as stubborn as usual.

Bella didn't comment, just kept on packing.

'Dare I hope you've come to your senses and are going to meet up with Andrei in Europe somewhere? It is summer over there, isn't it? If truth be told, I still can't fathom why you left him in the first place.'

Exasperation finally had Bella's head lifting, her glare more than a little angry. 'I didn't actually *leave* Andrei, Mum. We never lived together. I broke up with him because he was sleeping with other women at the same time as he was sleeping with me.'

'So you said. But truly, Bella, all seriously wealthy men have wandering eyes. And Andrei isn't just wealthy. He's a billionaire many times over. I read on the internet that he's just opened the most luxurious hotel in the world in Istanbul. Just think what kind of life you could have as his wife. He doesn't care about those other girls. It's you he pursued and wanted. You he would have proposed to, in the end.'

'No, he wouldn't have, Mum. Andrei's not the marrying kind.'

'Which is why I advised you to get pregnant. He would have married you then. A proud man like that would not have wanted to have an illegitimate child.'

Bella shook her head, thinking ruefully she should have told her mother the truth about Andrei. Yes, he was proud but was also totally selfish with absolutely no conscience. He'd fallen in lust with her when he'd seen her on stage one night in New York, pursuing her quite ruthlessly— and romantically—till she'd given in and gone to bed with him. At the time, she'd actually thought he loved her, and vice versa.

Unfortunately, their sex life was not a great success. Her fault, of course. It was always her fault; all of her lovers over the years—and there'd been a lot less than the tabloids suggested—having grown bored with her after a relatively short while. None of them could believe that she was actually quite shy in the bedroom. That was why she'd been a virgin till she was twenty-one, and why it always took a very determined admirer to seduce her.

When Bella had confronted Andrei with his unfaithfulness last year—his cavorting on the deck of his yacht with some female had been all over the gossip rags—he'd claimed that her *lack of passion* was why he had to have other women. He'd said he'd grown tired of her refusing to do all the erotic and exotic things he craved. But he would put up with her being somewhat boring in bed, he'd added, because he loved having a woman of her exquisite beauty on his arm in public. He'd even offered to buy her an apartment in Paris, if she would overlook his other mistresses and continue to go out with him. He'd actually been shocked when she'd told him their relationship—such as it was—was over. Andrei was not used to rejection from the opposite sex.

Of course, if Bella *had* told her mother all that, she would have said that she'd been a fool not to at least accept the apartment in Paris.

She was indomitable, her mother. Indomitable and dominating and downright infuriating, with a moral compass that was as suspect as Andrei's. Bella had grown up thinking Dolores was wonderful: a single mother who'd become estranged from her own family when she'd fallen pregnant during a working holiday overseas; supposedly seduced by a married Swedish chap she'd met on the snowfields of Switzerland. She'd refused to tell her disgusted parents the father's name, refused to have an abortion, then refused to live under their roof by their rules. Bella had admired that. If it were true, that was. She'd come to believe in recent times that maybe a lot of what Dolores had told her over the years might not have been strictly true. Still, it was true that Dolores had worked hard to give her daughter everything she'd needed. She'd even managed to budget her meagre wage as a receptionist to pay for dance and singing lessons. Though not with the kind of teacher she'd wanted for her talented Isabel.

So when a new boss had arrived on the scene, an Italian widower who'd been sent out to Sydney by his father to head the Australian branch of the family's import business, Dolores had seen the answer to all her problems. From photographs Bella had seen, Dolores had been a very attractive woman back then. Poor Alberto hadn't stood a chance, and soon Dolores had acquired a husband able to provide everything for his new stepdaughter that Dolores had wanted. Not only the best private tuition money could buy but also enrolment at a top school that specialised in the performing arts.

And the rest, as they said, was history.

Bella looked at her mother and wished she didn't still love the woman. Impossible not to, she supposed. She was her mother. On top of that, she knew Dolores did love Bella back, even if she was a pain in the neck.

'Mum,' she said firmly. 'I am not going to Europe to meet up with Andrei. Neither am I going to tell you where I'm going, except to say that I am going alone. Now I want you to leave this room ASAP. If you don't, I will pick you up bodily and carry you out.' Which she could. All those years of dancing had made Bella very strong. She was also a good eight inches taller than her mother, who barely topped five feet. Bella had obviously inherited her height and fair colouring from her Swedish father.

'Well, *really*!' Dolores exclaimed with a huff and a puff. 'There's no need to get nasty. I don't need telling twice when I'm not wanted. Just don't come crawling back to me the next time you need a place to run to.' And she stormed off.

Just in time too, Bella's phone ringing less than ten seconds after Dolores had slammed the bedroom door.

Relief flooded Bella when she saw it was Sergio calling. Relief and excitement. Already she was looking forward to seeing him again; to being in the company of someone she could relax with.

'Sergio,' she answered with pleasure in her voice. 'I've been waiting for you to call. As luck would have it, I've been able to get a flight which leaves Mascot late this afternoon.'

'That was quick,' he said.

'Yes, well, flying first class does have its advantages.

But there's still two stopovers. One in Singapore and one in Rome. I won't arrive in Milan for simply ages.'

His silence on the other end of the line worried her for a moment. 'You still want me to come, don't you?'

'Oh, definitely,' he said. 'I'm very much looking forward to it.'

Bella smiled. It was good that he actually wanted her to come. She didn't like to think he'd said yes out of pity for her.

'It will be good to catch up,' she said. 'I'll want to hear about everything you've been up to over the past decade or so. I know we ran into each other a few years back but we didn't actually talk much. I presume you've been successful at whatever you've been doing. You looked very impressive that night. But then you always were frightfully clever.'

'I've done all right for myself over the years,' he said with a modesty she wasn't used to in men. Usually they couldn't wait to brag. 'As have you, Bella. Impossible not to know about your successes when your life is lived in the spotlight. But let's not waste time exchanging personal details over the phone. I'd much rather do that when I see you in the flesh. Now I suggest you text me the time of your arrival when you get closer to Milan airport—at your last stopover, perhaps—and I will arrange for a car to pick you up. What name will you be travelling under? Not Bella, I hope.'

'Good God, no. I booked the seat under the name of Isabel Cameron. I wasn't always known as just Bella, you know.'

'Yes, I know. You were just Isabel when we first met.'

'So I was. But you used to call me Izzie. Till Mum told you not to. She said it was an awful nickname. She even complained about it to your father, do you remember?'

'I remember. Papa agreed with her and told me that if I had to shorten your name, I should call you Bella.'

Bella smiled at the memory. 'Which is hardly much shorter. But I did like it, especially after your father said it meant beautiful in Italian.'

'And wars.'

'What?'

'Bella is also the plural of *bellum*, meaning war in Latin.'

'Oh. I didn't know that. Anyway, Sergio, if you're worried about people recognising me, then don't. Once I put on a wig and glasses, no one ever recognises me. Tell the driver to hold up a sign with Dolores Cameron on it.'

'Fine,' he said crisply.

'You are *sure* about this, Sergio?' she asked, suddenly worried that she was imposing. 'I mean I could stay at one of the local hotels instead.'

'Don't be silly,' he said. 'I always did like your company.'

'Did you really? I always thought I drove you mad, dragging you away from your studies to watch me perform all the time.'

'You were an incorrigible little attention seeker, I have to admit,' he said, a smile in his voice. 'But you were also very talented. Watching you sing and dance was no hardship. Playing you at basketball, however, was a bit of a trial, especially after you cried when you didn't win.'

'I did not cry!' she protested.

'Yes, you did. The first time we played. After that, I let you win occasionally.'

She laughed. 'And I always thought I'd won fair and square.'

'Nothing in life is fair and square, Bella,' he said on a suddenly serious note.

'True,' she agreed, thinking of all the skulduggery that

went on in the entertainment industry. 'I'd better go, Sergio,' she added with some reluctance. She'd really enjoyed talking to him and reminiscing about old times. Happier times. Once again, Bella regretted not having kept in contact with Sergio after the divorce. Still, no use crying over spilt milk. They were in contact now and she aimed not to let him get away again. She could use a big brother in her life, someone who would always give her good advice, someone who didn't have a secret agenda of his own. 'I'll text you when I get to Rome.'

'Excellent. Oh, and, Bella…'

'What?'

'Don't forget. Don't tell anyone where you're going, or who you're staying with.'

'Don't worry, I won't. *Ciao*,' she finished up on an excited note, then hung up.

CHAPTER FIVE

SERGIO PLACED HIS phone on the bedside table, letting out a long sigh as he lay back against the pillows, his conscience urging him to change his mind about the course he'd set in motion tonight. But it was too late, of course. Way too late. He'd passed the point of no return the moment Bella had asked him to let her rent the villa.

He had to see this through, even if it was a disaster waiting to happen. For already Sergio suspected that seducing Bella might have consequences that would be not so easily dismissed.

Not a pregnancy. He wasn't stupid enough to let that happen. He was thinking of emotional consequences. The last thing he wanted to do was fall in love with her. Falling in lust with Bella was bad enough. But he could survive that. Hell, he had survived it. Just. Falling in love with her, however, was another ball game.

And it could happen, especially if he was going to spend so much time with her.

Then don't spend too much time with her, Sergio, came the brutally logical advice. Once you get her into your bed, go to Milan to work during the day and only come home to the villa at night.

Good thinking, Sergio.

Which only leaves the problem of getting her into your bed in the first place.

Easier said than done.

Clearly, she still thinks of you as her big brother; that rather quiet, introverted boy she first met. First impressions did tend to stick. He would have to make sure that, this time, she saw nothing of that boy. This time, Bella had to see someone very different. Not a totally bad boy. Sergio suspected he would not be able to bring off such a radical change in character with conviction. But there was room for a little wickedness and a lot of boldness.

He took some confidence from Bella's comment that she'd found him impressive when she'd seen him at that party a few years back. Though of course he'd been wearing a tux that night. Women often found a man impressive looking in a tux. Sergio needed Bella to be impressed by him *out of* his tux. He had a good body. Well shaped and well toned, with olive skin and surprisingly little body hair for an Italian. He also had an impressive package, a genetic blessing that women seemed to like. A lot. They might say size didn't matter but he'd found that, on the whole, the opposite was true.

Sergio sucked in sharply as he envisaged how it would feel, having sex with Bella. His body started envisaging it too. Damn. Now he would have trouble sleeping. Yet he had an early start tomorrow, even earlier than his original plans for this Friday. He'd been going to spend the whole day in the franchise's head office, thanking the staff for all their hard work as well as preparing them for the handover to their new bosses next Monday. Impossible now. All he could afford was a few hours in the morning. Unfortunate, but he would soften his abrupt departure by giving them the rest of the day off and paying in advance for them to have a handover party at a local pub.

Sergio hated cutting and running, but he had no option. He needed to get to Lake Como, pronto, the villa having been unoccupied for some time, Sergio not having darkened its doorstep since Easter. He knew Maria would have kept the place clean, but it might need an extra spruce up. She also needed to be told that a guest was coming to stay.

He would not tell her his guest's identity in advance, however. Just that it was a female friend. He didn't want her inadvertently leaking the information that Bella was coming to stay. And she might. Maria was a big fan of Bella's, a factor that had irked Sergio over the years. Maria had loved Dolores's beautiful daughter. Doted on her. Spoiled her, even. She had never forgotten her and had obviously found pleasure in Bella's success.

Maria was going to be very excited when he finally revealed who the mystery guest was, Sergio realised with some frustration, this troubling thought swiftly followed by another. How on earth was he going to seduce Bella right under Maria's nose without her finding out?

Impossible. Hell on earth! He'd backed himself into a corner here. Hardly an unusual situation where Bella was concerned. That creature had been nothing but trouble since the first day he'd clapped eyes on her.

No, no, Sergio, be honest here. The trouble didn't start till her sixteenth-birthday party when she'd emerged like a butterfly from a cocoon, blowing him away with her grace, her grown-up beauty and her devastating sex appeal. He hadn't been back to Sydney for several months; university life—and the sophistication of Rome—having more appeal than staying in a house run by a woman he disliked intensely. But Bella's birthday had coincided with his mid-year break in June, and his father had insisted he come home for the celebration, after which they would all fly to Lake Como for their annual holiday. The last time he'd seen Bella on the previous Christmas, she'd been a skinny schoolgirl in a ponytail and braces.

She hadn't been skinny that night. And her braces had been long gone. Instead, she'd worn make-up and the most exquisite party dress. White, of course. Dolores had known to dress her daughter in white, the colour making her look like an exquisite angel. Unfortunately, a sexy angel as well.

Yet Sergio had felt sure she was still a virgin. Dolores would have seen to that.

So Sergio had been startled when Bella had come up to him and demanded a birthday kiss.

'You'll have to do, Sergio,' she'd said without a hint of flirtation. 'A girl has to be kissed on her sixteenth birthday and you're the only male here, other than Papa. And he doesn't count.'

Sergio hadn't been ready for the effect on him when she'd gone up on tiptoe and pressed her mouth to his. For a split second, he'd been tempted to yank her hard against him, to part her innocent lips and plunge his tongue inside. *He* certainly hadn't been an innocent at twenty-one, not after two and a half years at university. But he'd resisted the devil's urging just in time, keeping the kiss to a platonic peck, which had obviously disappointed Bella, if her pout had been anything to go by.

Well, she's not an innocent now, he reminded himself as he rose and headed for the bathroom. Time you stopped having cold showers and started having what you've always wanted.

Which was Bella herself, in his bed and at his mercy.

CHAPTER SIX

EXCITEMENT AND ANTICIPATION built in Bella the closer she got to the villa. Not long now, she thought eagerly, catching glimpses of the lake through the tall trees.

Suddenly, she no longer felt tired, a burst of adrenalin firing her blood, forcing it to run less sluggishly through her veins. When she'd first exited the plane in Milan, she'd been absolutely wrecked, having managed only the briefest of dozes between stopovers. Unbelievably, she'd forgotten to bring her sleeping tablets with her, which meant she was in for a few sleepless nights at best.

Insomnia was the very devil. Bella hated tossing and turning in bed all night. Hated the negative thoughts that besieged her at such times. Hated the feeling of loneliness, which had been getting worse lately. Still, with a bit of luck the fresh air and change of scene would do what no sleeping tablet could achieve. Make her relax. Make her unwind. Make her work out what she really wanted in life. Because, quite frankly, she wasn't so sure any more.

There'd been a time when she'd thought she could have it all. An exciting and challenging career on the stage, with a devoted and supportive husband waiting in the wings to take her home afterwards to their lovely home and two happy children. A boy and girl, of course. Nothing but perfection in Bella's dream world.

It had come as a shock to her as she'd turned thirty last week that she wasn't even close to living that dream existence, with no hopes of achieving it any time in the near future. Okay, so she still had an exciting and challenging career. On paper. But it didn't feel as exciting and challenging any more. It just felt like hard work.

As for the idea of a devoted and supportive husband waiting in the wings… That was a pipe dream! Such a man simply did not exist. Men weren't devoted or supportive. At least, the ones she was attracted to weren't. They'd all been selfish, arrogant and only wanted her as a notch on their belt, or a status symbol, never as a wife. As for children… Bella knew she could have a baby if she wanted. You didn't need a husband for that these days. Just a sperm donor. She'd actually considered it—for about thirty seconds, the thought of being a single mother having no appeal whatsoever. She wanted her child—or children—to have a father as well as a mother, a man who actually loved and supported her, and who was hands-on with parenting.

'Almost there, Signorina Cameron,' the driver said, startling her out of her introspection.

The driver hadn't been a talker, thank heavens. But he spoke perfect English, with not too heavy an Italian accent. His name was Luigi and he was about fifty.

'Yes, I'm beginning to recognise things. I've been here before. Though not for several years.'

'It has not changed. Lake Como. Italy…it does not change much.'

'No,' she agreed warmly. 'That is part of its charm.'

The car pulled into a familiar gravel driveway, coming to a halt in front of tall wooden gates connected to a high stone wall. The gates looked new. The stone wall was not.

'Signor Morelli died last year,' Luigi told her in sombre tones as he pointed a remote controller at the gate.

'Yes, I know. I went to his funeral.'

Luigi frowned at her in the rear-vision mirror. 'You are not a relative.'

'No. Just a friend.'

'Ah.' He nodded sadly. 'I miss him. I was his driver for the last year of his life. He was a good man.'

'Yes,' Bella choked out. 'He was.'

'His son is a good man too.'

'He certainly is,' Bella agreed, glad to get off the subject of Alberto's death.

She was almost relieved when the gates were finally open and Luigi's attention was occupied with negotiating the Mercedes slowly round the crunchy gravel driveway that encircled a huge stone-edged fountain. As a child Bella had been shocked by the flagrant nudity of the three statues at the centre of the fountain. She still found the male statue slightly confronting. His sexual equipment was decidedly larger than normal, which possibly explained the looks of awe on his two female companions. Sergio's grandfather—who'd been alive and well when Bella had first holidayed at the villa—had claimed that the model for the male statue was a distant ancestor of his who'd built the villa in the sixteenth century. A myth, Sergio had told her later that same day, explaining that the villa had been a monastery back then, the Morelli family not buying it till late in the nineteenth century. The fountain—despite looking centuries old—was a later addition, built just after the First World War.

'You will learn, dear Izzie,' Sergio had confessed quietly with a rueful smile, 'that Italian men are given to boasting and bragging.'

Bella smiled at the memory. Not that she agreed with Sergio entirely. Yes, *some* Italian men liked to boast and brag. Sergio's grandfather had been of that ilk and his father to a lesser degree. Alberto had certainly liked showing off his attractive new wife and his pretty little stepdaughter. Sergio, however, didn't seem to have the need to impress others. Some people would have shouted to the rooftops that they were having the darling of Broadway as a guest in their home. But not Sergio. He'd insisted she tell no one where she was going, not even her mother.

Which suited Bella admirably, peace and privacy her priorities at the moment. She did wonder, however, if he'd told Maria that she was coming to stay.

Bella was still mulling over this question when the car came to a halt at the back entrance to the villa, the woman herself emerging through one of the heavy iron doors, her wide welcoming smile instantly answering that question.

Bella's somewhat world-weary heart lifted anew at the sight of her. Why, she'd hardly changed at all! A little plumper perhaps but still with that wonderfully happy face, glossy black hair and dancing dark eyes. When Maria hurried down the stairs and held her arms out wide, Bella climbed from the car straight into the warmest, most welcoming hug she'd had in years.

When Maria exclaimed, 'Oh, it is so good to see you again, Dolores!' Bella pulled back and almost burst out laughing. Just in time she kept a poker face, understanding that this was all for Luigi's benefit. Clearly, Maria knew full well who she was, despite the red wig and dark glasses she wore as a disguise.

Bella waited patiently whilst Luigi collected her luggage and carried it inside, after which she thanked him profusely and gave him a generous tip—she'd changed some money in Rome whilst waiting for the next leg of her flight. When he handed her his business card—in case she needed to be driven somewhere whilst she was here—she popped it in her jeans pocket then waved him off. Once he was safely gone, she whipped off the glasses and red wig and shook her fair hair free.

'Can I be called Bella now?' she asked Maria, who giggled in that delightfully girlish way Bella remembered.

'Sì. But is it allowed, now you are rich and famous?'

Bella gave her a look of mock reproach. 'If you start

that nonsense I will have to speak to your employer. Which reminds me, where is Sergio? Is he here yet?'

'*Sì*. He is helping Carlo with the garden and the pool. We did not know Sergio was to come here till later in July, so things have been a bit…what you say…neglectful? He said to tell you to go find him after you arrive.'

Bella smiled. She loved the way Maria spoke. Loved her Italian accent. Loved her little mistakes with English words. It was charming. She was charming. This whole place was charming.

'Oh, Maria!' she said with a deeply contented sigh. 'You've no idea how happy I am to be here.'

'Not as happy as Sergio. He is most…excited.'

Bella suspected Maria hadn't got that word right. Sergio was not the excitable type. Never had been. As much as she admired his self-contained persona, Bella found his tendency to be slightly straitlaced a touch irritating. Bella had never forgotten the night of her sixteenth birthday when she'd boldly asked him to kiss her. Bold for her, since she wasn't at all bold when it came to the opposite sex. But all the girls from her class had been there at the party. Several of them had even drooled over Sergio, who'd turned up looking very hot and hunky compared to the boys at school. One of the girls had actually dared her to go and kiss him, so she had. And what had he done? Stiffened all over then given her a one-second peck which had been both humiliating and rather hurtful, considering she'd thought she looked quite hot herself that night.

No, Sergio was not the excitable type. He certainly wasn't a typical hot-blooded Italian male. A good man, though, as the driver said.

'I might freshen up before I go find him,' Bella said, linking arms with Maria and steering her inside out of the heat. She'd forgotten how hot it could get here in the summer. 'What room have you put me in?'

'Sergio said you were to have one of the rooms next to his. He is in the master bedroom.'

Of course, Bella thought. He was master of the house now.

In the old days all children—even Sergio—had slept on the top floor of the villa, in bedrooms which didn't have the size or the luxury of the bedrooms on the middle floor, where all three rooms had en-suite bathrooms and French doors that opened out onto a wide, cool balcony. The master bedroom, which was central to the three, was extra large with a king-sized four-poster bed and the most decadent bathroom Bella had ever seen. All black marble and a huge sunken spa bath.

'Do I have a choice of which bedroom?' she asked as they mounted the stone staircase that led up to the first floor.

Maria shrugged. 'It is no matter. They have both been freshly cleaned. You choose.'

'Perhaps the one with the gold bedspread, then.'

Which was how Bella came to be unpacking in the room where her mother and Alberto had once slept when they had stayed there all those years ago, a delightful room whose décor was cream and gold and which Bella had always admired. It hadn't changed over the years, she thought as she dispensed with her too-hot jeans and pulled out a cool wrap-around dress made in the softest silk. The lovely antique furniture was the same, as was the gold-embossed wallpaper and the semi-transparent curtains that blew softly in the breeze from the lake. The bathroom was just as beautiful, Bella thought as she put her hair up in a loose knot and had a quick shower, the floor and walls covered in a cream marble with gold veins running through it. The fittings were all gold, the cream towels thick and soft. Once dried and dressed, Bella decided not to bother with make-up. Or with any further titivating. She was on holiday, after all. And the paparazzi had no idea she was here.

She might have lain down for a sleep—the big soft bed beckoned—but politeness insisted she find Sergio and tell him of her arrival. Maria had said that Sergio hadn't been expecting her for another hour or two yet. Understandable. When her plane had set down in Rome Bella had been told that the flight to Milan had been delayed an hour, with her text to Sergio informing him of the fact. But the plane had actually taken off only half an hour late with the pilot making up good time with favourable winds. So she'd arrived at the villa earlier than the mid-afternoon Sergio would have anticipated.

When Bella emerged from the bathroom, she headed out onto the balcony, which gave an excellent view, not just of the lake, but the villa's lovely garden and grounds. Glancing down and around in search of Sergio, her eyes immediately landed on a man who was vacuuming the pool. He was tall and dark-haired, wearing nothing but a pair of brief swimming trunks, showing off an impressive physique.

Dear heaven, she thought as she ogled the way his back muscles moved underneath his gorgeous skin. Not fair skin like her own, but beautifully bronzed in the way only men of Mediterranean genes achieved without using artificial methods. He was beautiful all over, she thought, with broad shoulders and a nicely shaped head, crowned with thick black hair that gleamed in the sunshine. She could not stop staring down at him, her lonely heart envying Maria for ensnaring herself such a hunky husband. For this had to be Carlo.

But no sooner had this thought entered her head than *Carlo* lifted *his* head and looked straight up at her, his very familiar eyes bringing a gasp to her lips.

For it wasn't Carlo but Sergio; the supposedly straitlaced, coolly contained Sergio, looking every inch the hot-blooded Italian his heritage demanded he be, his hair longer than she remembered, his chin covered with a dark stubble that looked very macho on him. Very…sexy.

'What are you doing here this early?' he said, smiling up at her.

Bella struggled to put aside her shock, both at Sergio's near-naked beauty, plus her reaction to it. She didn't want to be attracted to Sergio; didn't want that kind of distraction, or complication. She'd come here for some much-needed rest. The last thing she needed was to be plagued by awkward feelings that were both unexpected and unwanted.

Damn it all, I do not want this, Bella thought with a burst of true frustration.

Hopefully, once Sergio put some clothes back on, she would be able to look at him and feel nothing but what she'd always felt for him, which was admiration and affection. Not sexual attraction.

Yet it was very much sexual attraction that was at this moment rattling her composure. She couldn't stop staring at him, her heartbeat picking up its pace as it did just before she went on stage some nights. When her face began to flush with an embarrassing heat, Bella harnessed every ounce of willpower she owned and returned his smile.

'The pilot put his foot down between Rome and Milan,' she told him, her casual tone amazing her. Maybe she was as good an actress as Charlie said she was.

'I see,' Sergio replied. 'Look, I'm almost finished here, which is just as well,' he added ruefully. 'I haven't been this hot in living memory. Go down to the kitchen and get Maria to open a bottle of my favourite Chablis, will you? She knows the one. We can share it down here on the terrace. I'll just have a quick swim first,' he added and walked down to the far end of the pool, where he stood there with his legs slightly apart and his arms by his sides before glancing up at her again. 'I'd suggest you join me in the pool but I imagine you're feeling jet-lagged after such a long flight.'

'I am tired,' she managed to reply, thinking she hadn't felt this hot in living memory either. Or ever, for that matter.

Despite her knowing she should stop ogling Sergio, her gaze kept roving over his near-naked body, marvelling at how utterly gorgeous he was without clothes on. Better looking than any man she'd ever been to bed with. He was perfectly shaped, his broad-shouldered chest tapering down into a slim waist, a tight butt and long, strong legs. He also had just the right amount of muscle. Whatever Sergio had been doing over the years he hadn't become a couch potato. Which begged the question of what *had* he been doing with himself since their parents' divorce? She doubted he'd been working in the family firm if he was living in London. The Morelli business was in Milan. Unless, of course, Alberto had given Sergio charge of a London branch, the way *his* father had sent *him* to Sydney all those years ago.

This train of thought momentarily distracted Bella from her embarrassing ogling, curiosity over what Sergio did for a living making her agree to go in search of Maria, and that bottle of wine. At least, she told herself it was curiosity. It couldn't possibly be because she wanted to see him up closer, or wanted to find out, not so much about his career path, but about his personal life.

By the time Bella settled herself at the table on the terrace, however, she admitted to herself that that was exactly what she wanted to find out. But to what end, Bella? she asked herself as she surreptitiously watched Sergio surging through the water with effortless ease. You've come here to Lake Como for peace and quiet, not to have an affair with your long-lost stepbrother. Which is what might happen if you start flirting with him. Bella knew men found her desirable. Some claimed to find her irresistible.

Till they get you into bed, that is, came the stark reminder. Then, after a while, they don't find you quite so desirable, or irresistible. Face it, Bella, you *are* a bore in bed. A failure. You might be beautiful to look at but you are incapable of being truly turned on. Your finding Sergio physically attractive means nothing. You've always been attracted to tall, dark and handsome. Unfortunately, that attraction never seems to translate into passion, the kind that bypasses shy and forces you to lose control.

Bella had always envied the way her lovers sometimes lost control. It would be wonderful, just once, to lose control. But she never had. Perhaps she never would. Or could. Maybe it was something she'd inherited from her mother, whose iron will and self-control bordered on obsessive. Maybe her shyness when naked was not shyness at all but an unwillingness to let down the in-built defences that came from being the daughter of an embittered and cynical woman. Bella had no doubt her mother loved her but it was a warped kind of love. Possessive and controlling and manipulative.

It was at this depressing point in her train of thought that Sergio stopped at the end of the pool less than three metres from the table Bella was sitting at.

'Time to get out,' he said, bringing her attention to his face; his sexily unshaven face.

Bella smothered a sigh of exasperation at her ongoing thoughts. Common sense demanded she drag her gaze away from Sergio, but she could not. So she watched, heart racing, as he placed his two palms on the flat surrounds and pushed upwards, his biceps bulging as he propelled himself out of the pool in a single leap. He landed like a big cat on the flagstones, water streaming down his chest as he straightened then slicked his hair back with large wet hands. Bella's breath caught in her throat as she just stared at him, her hungry gaze raking over his gorgeous male body from top to toe.

Thank heavens Maria appeared with the ice bucket and glasses at that point, Bella glad to have an excuse to turn away and help her. Not that looking away from Sergio achieved all that much. It hadn't taken more than a couple of seconds for her to spy what was on display within the confines of his tightly fitted shorts. Not only was Sergio hotter looking without clothes on than any man she'd ever been with, but he was bigger. Quite a bit bigger, if her eyes hadn't deceived her.

Her mouth dried as she imagined how it would feel to be made love to by a man of such impressive proportions. Though *making love* was hardly what she had in mind. The sexual fantasy suddenly filling Bella's head was not romantic, or gentle. In it, Sergio was taking her without foreplay, without tenderness, without lies about loving. She did not want to be told he loved her. She just wanted sex. Raw, naked, animal sex.

Not just attraction this time, Bella accepted shakily as she picked up the bottle of wine that sat in the ice bucket in the middle of the table. This was lust. The most famous of the seven deadly sins. Infamous for its power to seduce and to destroy; for banishing consciences and making fools of the most sensible people.

As much as Bella craved the scenario of losing control, she'd hoped she would be in love at the time, not in lust. When she'd arrived here, she certainly hadn't envisaged falling in lust with Sergio. The possibility that she might make a fool of herself with him truly horrified her. By the time he wrapped a towel around his hips and joined her at the table, she'd managed to banish that wicked fantasy to the far reaches of her mind, determined not to give in to urges that were not very nice. Already they threatened to spoil her holiday, something she refused to allow. She needed this break, quite desperately. What she did not need was to fall victim to feelings that were strictly sexual and superficial. She did not love Sergio. She didn't even know him any more. If truth be told, he was virtually a stranger. The boy she'd once known and liked had become a man. A man with his own life and his own plans. A man who undoubtedly already had a woman in his life. Only a fool would imagine otherwise.

After the break-up with Andrei last year, Bella had vowed to stop being a fool where men were concerned. Time to test that vow!

Gathering herself, she schooled her face into a mask of indifference to Sergio's near nakedness and poured him a glass of wine.

'You swim very well,' she said coolly as she handed him the glass. 'But then, you always did.'

CHAPTER SEVEN

As Sergio reached to take his glass, he looked deep into her lovely but very cool blue eyes. Yet they hadn't been cool a few seconds ago. They'd been hot and hungry as they stared at him. He'd been sure of it.

Not a sign of anything now, however. She was all cool sophistication as she sat there, looking cripplingly desirable in a silky floral sundress. She was too thin, of course. Women who lived their lives in the spotlight were always too thin in Sergio's opinion. Perversely, Bella's slenderness only made her more desirable, giving her tall, willowy body a fragility that was both appealing and provocative. Her porcelain skin was free of make-up, her glorious blonde hair up in a style that showed off her long, elegant neck and pretty shell-like ears. She wasn't wearing lipstick, but then her lips didn't need lipstick, her mouth full and lush and pink in its natural state.

Sergio's gut tightened as he imagined kissing that mouth. And that neck. And those ears. When he started imagining a whole lot more, he told himself to get a grip.

'I seem to recall you were quite the little fish as well,' he said, and took a welcome swallow of the cold wine. The swim had achieved only marginal success when it came to dampening the sexual heat Bella always evoked in him. He'd still been half erect when he exited the pool, and was now back in full flight, an uncomfortable state of affairs given the restrictions of wet Lycra.

But he was used to pain where Bella was concerned.

Sergio was contemplating how to handle the rest of the

day when Maria appeared on the terrace with one of the house phones.

'The Contessa,' she said quietly to Sergio as she handed the receiver to him.

Sergio was momentarily annoyed at the interruption, till he saw Bella's eyebrows lift. Nothing heightened a woman's interest, he'd sometimes found, than the interest of another woman.

'Excuse me a moment,' he said to Bella as he lifted the phone to his ear. 'Claudia,' he said, putting a warm lilt into his voice. 'So nice of you to call.'

'You naughty man,' the Countess chided. 'You come to stay and you don't tell me in advance. I would have organised a dinner party in honour of your arrival if I'd known.'

'How kind of you. But I'm not in the mood for major socialising. How about a dinner for just the two of us instead? Tomorrow night, perhaps? Eight o'clock suit you?'

'*Sì.* Eight o'clock would be lovely. I will have Angela cook you something special. And I'll open the Chianti Giovanni laid down in the cellar before he died.'

Which was almost ten years ago, meaning the Chianti would be fantastic to drink by now. 'I will look forward to it. Must go, Claudia. I've been cleaning out the pool and I am in desperate need of a shower.'

He hung up swiftly before she could ask why he was doing Carlo's job. Impossible to explain that he'd *wanted* to be cleaning the pool when Bella arrived, the driver having texted him the approximate time of their arrival before he'd left Milan. His plan had been for Bella to see him without the cloak of a suit, certain that she would find his body attractive. He had a good body, he knew. Also, if history was anything to go by, Bella had a penchant for tall men with olive skin and dark hair. He was confident that his plan had worked, her eyes eating him up more than once.

But Bella was a sophisticated and very beautiful woman.

A successful woman. She didn't need to chase after a man, even one she found physically attractive. She would be used to men chasing after her, sending her flowers and flattering her with words of admiration and desire. Sergio had thought of using such a method to seduce her, but decided against it, certain she would be bored with such obvious tactics. He wanted to be more original than that. Given the intimacy of their living in the same house, he was sure that a situation suited to seduction would present itself sooner or later.

'A countess, Sergio?' Bella said with a sardonic note in her voice. 'Does she have red hair, perhaps?'

Sergio frowned. 'Why would you say that?'

'A very attractive woman with red hair claimed your arm at your father's funeral whilst we were talking.'

Sergio couldn't honestly remember. But Bella did. Which was interesting.

'Claudia does have red hair. Yes. She's my next-door neighbour,' he added. 'Lives in a villa up on the hill to our left, which makes the Morelli villa look like a B & B. She's a very good neighbour. And a very good friend.'

'And is the Count a very good friend of yours as well?'

Sergio smiled. She *was* jealous. Clearly, she'd been put out by his agreeing to have dinner elsewhere so soon after she'd come to stay. Which was exactly why he'd suggested it, Sergio having decided off the cuff to follow one of the tactics Jeremy had suggested the other night.

Treat 'em mean and keep 'em keen.

'The Count died several years ago,' he informed a curious-faced Bella.

'I see,' Bella said, somewhat snippily.

She didn't see, of course. But that was all right. It suited Sergio's purpose that Bella believed Claudia was a merry widow and that tomorrow night he would be having the beautiful widow for afters. But Claudia had to be at least fifty-five, her plastic surgeon deserving a medal for the wonderful job he'd done on her over the years.

Maria showed up at the table at that point with two plates of bruschetta, Sergio grateful for the food. He'd already had lunch but it seemed like hours ago, his appetite sharpened by the physical work he'd been doing.

All his appetites were sharp at that moment.

'So are you going to tell me why you were so desperate to get away?' he asked Bella between bites.

Her eyes betrayed a momentary confusion as though she'd forgotten the reason for her flight. But then she laughed. A strange laugh. Almost bitter. Possibly ironic.

'It's difficult to put into words. I guess I'd just had enough of everything. Enough of work. And life. And men. Especially men,' she added with heavy emphasis.

Terrific, Sergio thought. Suddenly, his goal of seducing Bella just became even more difficult.

'I'm a man,' he said before he could think better of it.

'I know that, Sergio,' she said stiffly, her eyes closing momentarily as her shoulders lifted then sank. 'But you're... different.'

'Not as different as you might think, Bella,' he muttered, hating the way his conscience was suddenly prodding him.

'You wouldn't tell a woman you loved her just to get her into bed, would you?'

'No. I wouldn't.' As much as he might be tempted to...

'See? You're different from the amoral bastards I've been unfortunate enough to get mixed up with. You're a gentleman.'

'But no less a man. If I really wanted a woman, I might not always act the gentleman.'

'I don't believe that.'

'Then you're a fool,' he snapped, frustration making him impatient.

When he saw the hurt in her eyes his remorse was immediate.

'I apologise,' he said. 'That was uncalled for. But I'm not a saint, Bella, and you're a very beautiful woman.'

Their eyes met across the table, Sergio noting the instant panic in hers. He wasn't sure if that was good news or bad.

'M…maybe my staying here wasn't such a good idea, after all,' she stammered. 'I think it would be best if I booked into a hotel.'

Bad news, damn it all. Still, Sergio wasn't about to let Bella run away. He'd always known seducing her would be a challenge. But it would be impossible if she weren't under his roof.

'Don't be silly, Bella,' he said in a silky smooth voice, the one he used to negotiate difficult deals. 'I'm not about to make some crass pass the moment Maria goes home this evening. I might be between girlfriends right now but I am at an age where I can manage without sex for a mere month. So eat and drink up, then go have a much-needed nap.'

CHAPTER EIGHT

BUT THAT'S THE PROBLEM, Bella wailed to herself as she dropped her eyes from his to the food. Any attentions on your part *would* be welcome. And the pass can be as crass as you like. Tell me you want me. Right here and now. On this table or on the floor. I won't say no. I want you to strip off my panties and just do it. Without care. Without any words of love, or even liking.

Dear Lord, what was happening to her here? This wasn't *her*, this creature who wanted such appalling things; who suddenly *craved* them. Of course, it was all just in her head. It wasn't real. If Sergio actually made a pass at her, she'd probably run a mile.

But it wasn't entirely in her head, was it? The heat between her thighs was real. So were the pounding of her heart and the tightening of her nipples. Those things were very real. And very upsetting.

She had to get away. Maybe not right this second. But as soon as she could without offending Sergio. In a couple of days she would invent a phone call from Hollywood with an offer she couldn't refuse. Meanwhile, she would keep out of his corrupting presence as much as possible. Suddenly, his going to dinner tomorrow night with that Countess woman didn't bother her as much as it had, though she still hated the thought of his having sex with her. Which was ridiculous! Why shouldn't he have sex with her if he wanted to? As he said, he was between girlfriends at the moment.

But it was no use. Just the thought of Sergio having

sex with that woman sent a wave of black jealousy washing through her.

Her eyes lifted and collided with his, Bella fearful that he would see the guilty hunger in hers.

Flustered, she said the first thing she could think of. 'What time will dinner be tonight?'

'Whatever time you like,' he replied. 'I didn't want to ask Maria to cook. She's been working very hard the last two days, cleaning the villa from top to bottom. I thought we could stroll along to the village and have dinner there. Several new restaurants have sprung up since you were last here. But if you're too tired to go out, I could throw something together.'

'You can *cook*?'

He shrugged. 'I'm a bachelor living in the twenty-first century. Of course I can cook. If you call steak and salad cooking,' he added with a wickedly attractive grin.

Oh, God…

Bella didn't trust herself to behave if they had an intimate dinner alone in the villa. Far better they dined out in public. Dining out would also guarantee that Sergio would have some decent clothes on. Who knew what he would wear here at home? The weather was hot. Maybe he'd just put on some shorts, leaving his chest bare. His gorgeous, sexy chest.

'I don't mind steak and salad,' she said, dragging her lusty eyes away from that corrupting chest to top up her wine, 'but I think I would like to go out. Provided I get some sleep first.'

'Fine. I'm easy. You're not eating,' he pointed out.

'Oh. No. I'm not very hungry. Just tired and thirsty.' She swiftly lifted the wine glass to her lips and drained it dry, sighing as she put it back down on the table, hoping that the alcohol would dampen her desire and make her sleep. Scraping her chair back, she stood up, startled to find that her legs were decidedly wobbly. 'I think I will go up to my room now.'

'Take the plate with you,' he suggested. 'You need to eat, Bella.'

'Are you saying I'm too thin?' she snapped, having grown sensitive to comments about her eating habits in recent years. When she was stressed, she couldn't eat. On the rare occasions she felt happy, she ate with relish, her weight going up and down like a yo-yo. She often lost more than she should, however. At the moment, she was slightly underweight. But not dangerously so.

'You could afford to put on a few pounds,' he said.

Although the comment was honest, it still upset Bella.

'And you could afford to be a little more polite,' she shot back. 'I expect to be criticised by the media but not my friends.'

To give him credit, his expression was immediately remorseful. 'You're right,' he said. 'I'm sorry. I'm usually more tactful than that. I'm worried about you, that's all. As I said earlier, you are a very beautiful woman, Bella. You would be beautiful no matter what weight you were. But it's clear you've been working yourself too hard. You need to relax, and to eat, not just drink.'

'Might I remind you, Sergio,' she retorted, her dander right up now, 'that you are not my big brother any more. My welfare is not your concern. Neither is my weight. So spare me the lectures on eating and drinking. If I wanted to be lectured I would have stayed in Sydney with my mother. Now, if you don't mind, I'm going upstairs to have some much-needed rest.'

Sergio winced as he watched her flounce off.

Well done, Sergio. That's the way to seduce a woman. Tell her she's too skinny!

Sergio laughed a dry laugh. At least she recognised

that he wasn't her big brother any more. She'd called him a friend. That was a start. But it suddenly felt a long way from friend to lover.

Maria came out onto the terrace and glared down at the uneaten food.

'Leave it,' Sergio said when she went to pick up the plate. 'I'm hungry enough for two.' He always ate like a horse when he was stressed.

Maria made a tsk-tsk noise with her mouth. 'That girl... she is too thin.'

'I know,' Sergio said. 'I told her so.' And he took a big bite of bruschetta.

Maria stared at him as if he was mad. Which he was. Stark raving mad.

'You are *stupido*,' she said, waving her hands in the air. 'How you think you get Bella into bed if you say things like that?'

Sergio almost choked on his food. Still, he should have known that he wouldn't be able to deceive Maria. She was one smart woman. At least now he wouldn't have to hide his intentions from her. Or the evidence, if he was ever successful. Which at that moment seemed unlikely.

'How long have you known?' he asked her.

'That you are in love with Bella?' She shrugged her shoulders. 'I have always known. Ever since you were children. You become a different boy when she came into your life. She lit up your soul.'

Sergio laughed again. She certainly lit up something. But it wasn't his soul. 'I am not in love with Bella, Maria. I did love her when I was a boy. How could anyone not love her back then? But she is no longer the enchanting little girl she once was. She's grown up into a tough cookie with an all-consuming career and a string of lovers a mile long. She's also grown into the most desirable woman God ever put breath into. So yes, I would like to get her into bed. I won't deny it. But that's all I want.'

'You men,' Maria scoffed. 'You never know what you want, or what you feel. My Carlo. He thought the same, but once I am having his child, he saw the truth. That it is love all along.'

'Are you talking about me, *caro*?' the man himself said as he walked out onto the terrace.

Carlo was a handsome man with curly black hair and a carefree disposition. He'd had a roving eye in his younger years but was now a devoted family man, proving that people could change.

'*Sì*, Carlo,' Maria said, smiling at him. 'I was saying what a wonderful husband and *papà* you are.'

Carlo beamed. 'I do my best. I must away, Sergio. School will be out and those *bambinos* of mine, they are little devils.'

'Is the boat all ready to go?' Sergio asked.

He had set Carlo the task of cleaning his father's speedboat whilst he'd vacuumed the pool.

'*Sì*. I check the engine and clean everything till it shine.'

'Then go, by all means,' Sergio said, thinking how much Carlo's English had improved over the years. They never spoke Italian at the villa, Maria explaining that with the explosion of tourism at the lake they both needed to be able to speak perfect English. 'And many thanks. You are a very good worker, Carlo.'

'And you are a very good boss. *Ciao*.'

'But still a stupid one,' Maria said with rolling eyes once her husband was gone.

Sergio sighed. 'I get the point, Maria. You don't have to rub it in.'

She muttered something in Italian under her breath, then whirled and stalked off, leaving Sergio feeling disgusted with himself. Both Alex and Jeremy would have been disgusted too, if they'd witnessed the most classic *faux pas* of all *faux pas* when it came to seduction. Neither of them would have been so crass as to make a comment about a woman's weight.

It was all Bella's fault, of course. Whenever she entered his head, his brain got scrambled.

Think, Sergio. Think!

There were two courses of action he could take, he decided as he finished off the bruschetta and wine. He could adopt the patient approach. Just talk to her at first, like a friend. Ask her questions about her career. Show an interest in her life. Find out what she planned to do in the future. He'd often found that women liked men who were good listeners.

Alternatively, he could revert to the bad-boy approach, which would mean that the next time they were alone together, if the mood was right, he *would* make a pass. Not crass, of course. Something suave and sophisticated. Something original and clever. It would be a risk, but one worth taking. For Sergio suspected that he would quickly run out of patience with Bella sleeping in the bedroom next to his. *He* certainly wouldn't get much sleeping done.

Laughing ruefully at this last thought, he stood up, dumped the empty glasses in the wine bucket with the bottle, gathered up the plates and carried everything into the huge kitchen.

Maria glanced up from where she was busy writing some sort of list.

'What is so funny?' she asked.

'Life, Maria. Life,' he said as he put the bottle in the recycling bin and the rest in the dishwasher. 'Now go home. You've done enough for today. I don't want to see you till lunchtime tomorrow. And before you start arguing, Bella and I are quite capable of getting ourselves breakfast.'

'Have you booked the restaurant for dinner? It is Saturday night. Lots of people eating out.'

'No. But I will. We won't be eating till late. Bella is having a sleep first. Now go!' he ordered, waving her off.

She went with some reluctance, Sergio relieved to see her go. He was tired of talking. Tired of thinking. He'd go have a shower and a sleep too. If he could sleep, that was. Normally, drinking wine like that in the daytime made him drowsy. But today was not a normal day.

Sighing and shaking his head at the same time, Sergio headed for the stairs.

CHAPTER NINE

BELLA TOSSED AND TURNED on the bed, jet lag plus a lack of medication making sleep impossible.

Yet she needed to sleep, quite desperately. Needed some peace from the thoughts plaguing her. She still found it hard to believe that she had fallen in lust with Sergio. Okay, so he was an impressive-looking man now, with a truly gorgeous body, a far cry from the lanky, skinny teenager she'd known all those years ago. But he was still *Sergio*, her one-time big brother, a truly kind man who'd generously let her come and stay here, despite her having turned her back on him and his father after the divorce.

Amazingly, he didn't seem to hold any grudges against her; his manner over the phone had been quite warm and charming. She'd anticipated on the flight over that they would have a lovely time together, catching up on old times, totally relaxed in each other's company, Bella looking forward to asking Sergio's advice over what she should do with the rest of her life. She'd thought of him as sensible Sergio, not sexy Sergio.

She hadn't for a moment imagined that she would be instantly besieged by a desire for him so strong that it made staying here impossible. Tears threatened, tears of exhaustion and frustration. For she wanted to stay. And she wanted Sergio. What on earth was she going to do?

Have a hot shower for starters, dummy, came that exasperated voice in her head that often piped up when she was frazzled or at her wits' end. Or a cold one, if you can stand it. Just do something! Don't just lie there, moaning and groaning like some drama queen.

Gritting her teeth, Bella headed for the bathroom where she stood under some soothingly warm water for ages, uncaring that her hair was getting soaked. When she finally emerged she felt a little better, though she looked a mess. Her long blonde hair was not at its best when wet. It kinked and curled and stuck out everywhere. Sighing, she gave it a brief dry with the hairdrier, then wrapped it up on top of her head before putting her new white silk PJs back on. She'd bought them at Mascot airport whilst waiting for her flight to be called. Bought a bikini as well.

By the time she cleaned her teeth and returned to the bedroom, the sun had sunk very low in the sky, its rays slanting onto the balcony and bathing the bedroom in a soft light. When the curtains ballooned out with a puff of breeze, Bella found herself making her way out onto the balcony, hoping that her still-jumpy nerve-endings would be soothed by the sight of the lake. Water was supposed to have a soothing effect, wasn't it?

It was so beautiful, the lake, the water a dark blue-green colour, boats of all kind skimming over its near-smooth surface. Sailing boats. Speedboats. Ferries. Bella stood at the stone railing and watched the boats for a while, before lifting her gaze to the other side of the lake, where more magnificent villas dotted the shoreline, some of them half hidden by tall trees. Her eyes lifted to the mountains that stretched high into the clear blue sky, the highest peaks snow-capped despite it being summer. Despite the view her thoughts continued to return to Sergio.

'I see you can't sleep either,' the man himself said as he materialised next to her.

Bella steeled herself as she turned her head to look at him, guessing already that Sergio wasn't wearing any more clothes than he had earlier. She'd glimpsed bare arms as he'd reached out to grip the railing.

She'd been right. A lot of him was still bare. Bare arms. Bare chest. Bare legs and feet.

The black satin boxer shorts he was wearing weren't as revealing as his swimming shorts. But it was obvious that he was naked underneath them. Bella's PJs weren't much better, made up of shorts and a sleeveless shirt top with a low V neckline.

'I've been having trouble sleeping for some time,' she told him truthfully enough. She could hardly say that *he* was the reason. 'I usually take a sleeping tablet but I forgot to bring mine with me. You wouldn't have any, by any chance?' she added, sneaking another glance his way. Oh, Lord, what a masochist she was!

'Sorry,' Sergio replied. 'Don't believe in them. Not that I usually have a problem with insomnia. I work out quite a bit and swim a lot. On the odd occasion I can't sleep—like now—I try Mother Nature's sleeping tablet.'

Bella turned and stared at him, frustration making her voice sharp. 'Well, I'm sorry, Sergio, but I don't think a cup of chamomile tea is going to do the trick.'

He laughed, his dark eyes glittering with humour. And something else. Something smokingly hot.

'I wasn't suggesting chamomile tea. I was talking about sex. Don't you find that after an orgasm or two, you drop off to sleep quite easily?'

Bella didn't know what to say to that. She'd never had one orgasm, let alone two. She'd come close a few times— or thought she had—but had never experienced total satisfaction. Just total frustration.

'Yes, well, I'm between boyfriends at the moment,' was all she could think of to say.

He looked at her long and hard, and Bella's heart beat so fast she was sure he must hear it.

'You don't need a boyfriend to have sex, Bella. Just a man. You're welcome to use me, if you like. As I pointed out earlier, I'm a man,' he added, a devilish gleam in his eyes.

She just stared at him, her eyes wide with shock. Who would have believed that Sergio could be so...so...?

Bella could not find the right word. Sexy wasn't strong enough. Wicked was closer to the mark.

An image popped into her head, of how *big* he'd looked in those very revealing swimming trunks, and of how she'd tried to imagine what it would feel like, having a man of his size inside her. Her mouth dried at the thought, her heartbeat going truly haywire.

'You can't be serious!' she blurted out at last.

'I'm very serious.'

'But I...you...we...'

'Are not related in any way,' he finished for her. 'We never were. Look, I've always fancied you, Bella. Especially *after* you grew up and became all famous and gorgeous. If truth be told, most of the male population in the world fancies the beautiful Bella. So it won't be any hardship to make love to you.'

Bella gulped, shock and temptation having rendered her speechless. Not in her wildest dreams would she have thought Sergio would offer himself to her in such a fashion. She wanted to say yes. She really did. But finding that one little word was so hard.

'I don't usually go to bed with a man just to get some sleep,' she hedged.

He shrugged. 'There's always a first time for everything.'

'I...I don't know, Sergio,' she said, trying to find some reason—*any* reason—to say no, panic a heartbeat away. 'People say sex has a way of spoiling friendships.'

'Come now, Bella, it's not as though we live in each other's pockets. When this month is over, you'll wing your way back to New York and we probably won't see each other again for another decade.'

Bella frowned, not liking that thought one bit.

'What's that expression?' Sergio said with a wry smile, reaching out to take her by the shoulders and pull her towards him. 'Friends with benefits? That is what we can be, Bella. Friends with benefits.'

Bella made no comment. She couldn't. Because by then his mouth had covered hers.

CHAPTER TEN

SERGIO TRIED TO keep his head. Tried to take things slowly. But this was *Bella* he was finally kissing. Bella who was melting against him and moaning in that soft, sexy way women did when they were turned on. Any momentary worry he'd had that she might not respond to him was banished at the sound of that first little moan, his control banished at the same time. His hands shook as they lifted from her shoulders to clasp her cheeks, holding her face captive while he pried those luscious lips apart and sent his tongue deep into her mouth. She welcomed it avidly, her own tongue entwining with his in an erotic dance that had him fully erect in seconds.

His groan was half passion, half pain. With great reluctance he dragged his mouth away from hers, knowing that he needed a breather or he would never last the way he wanted to last. No way could he disappoint her. Not this first time. Not if he wanted Bella to want more than just a one-night stand.

'Wow, Bella,' he said lightly as he returned his hands to her shoulders. 'You are some kisser.' Of course, she'd had a lot of practice. Not a thought he relished. 'Unless you want to have sex out here on the balcony,' he went on drily, 'I suggest we adjourn to the bedroom.'

She blinked up at him, face flushed, eyes somewhat glazed.

'Bella?' he prompted when she said nothing. 'Your room or mine?'

She still didn't speak, seeming disoriented. Maybe she

hadn't expected to like kissing him as much as she obviously had. Whatever, Sergio wasn't about to let her go cold on the idea of having sex with him. So he bent and scooped her up into his arms and carried her swiftly into the master bedroom. She made no protest, though her eyes rounded when he laid her down on the black satin sheets that graced the king-sized bed.

She still didn't say anything.

'Look, if you're one of those women who don't like to talk during sex, then say so right now,' he said, deliberately using conversation to dampen the urgency of his own desire.

'I don't like to talk,' she said, her voice low and husky.

He shrugged. 'Pity, it's good to know what a woman likes or doesn't like, especially the first time.'

'I see,' she said, her lovely eyes clinging to his in a way that made him want to kiss her again. But he didn't dare.

'So is there anything you especially like?' he asked. 'Besides kissing, that is. I can see you like that.'

She frowned as though she was at a loss to answer. 'No...not...not really,' she said at last.

'Fine. What about things you don't like?'

A small smile pulled at her lips. 'I don't like to talk.'

He laughed. 'Right. No more talking.'

He didn't mind. He'd had his breather, his body back under control. Sort of.

Propping himself up on his left elbow, he reached to undo the top button of her silky top, telling himself all the while not to look at her breasts. Just get her undressed.

If only she hadn't gasped when he'd peeled the top open. If only she hadn't closed her eyes and tipped her head back on the pillows, the action lifting her breasts towards him in the most inviting fashion. Impossible not to look after that. Impossible not to touch.

She wasn't too thin at all. At least, her breasts weren't.

They were perfect, twin globes of pearly flesh with the sweetest, pinkest, pointiest nipples. They demanded to be licked and kissed, then sucked in deeply, all of which he did, uncaring of the danger to his control. She started whimpering, then thrashing her head from side to side on the pillow. Her hands found his head, her fingers winding their way through his hair, not to pull him away but to press him down closer and harder. She cried out when he abandoned her breasts to slide downwards, stripping off her bottom half as he went and tossing it aside. She voiced only the weakest protest when he pushed her legs apart. But there was no further protest once his mouth reached its target. She writhed, then bucked with pleasure, moaning and groaning as his tongue and fingers set up a twin attack on her most erogenous zones.

From that moment her orgasm was assured. As was his.

They came together. Yet not together, any dismay on Sergio's part put aside once he realised that this was only the beginning. She was his now, he thought as he moved to sit on the side of the bed. Sexually, at least. All he had to do was keep satisfying her and she would come back for more. For that was the nature of the beast.

At last, she opened her eyes and stared into his, her expression full of wonder.

'I had no idea it could be like that,' she said, sounding stunned.

'Like what?' he said, his still-hungry gaze roving over her delicious nakedness.

She immediately closed her legs, looking more than a little confused. 'I thought... I thought I had to be in love to...to...you know...'

Sergio was taken aback that a thirty-year-old woman of Bella's experience could be so naïve.

'Sometimes, sex without love is better,' he told her, thinking he wouldn't really know since he'd never been in love. 'You can concentrate on the physical rather than the emotional. Emotions complicate things.'

'You're probably right,' she murmured. 'Have you ever been in love, Sergio?'

'No,' he returned abruptly, annoyed that Maria had put silly thoughts of love into his head earlier. He was not in love with Bella. Definitely not. 'Now I have to go to the bathroom for a sec. Then we'll get down and dirty and have some real sex.'

CHAPTER ELEVEN

'DEAR HEAVEN,' Bella whispered to herself after Sergio closed the bathroom door behind him.

What had happened to the Bella who hated being naked in front of a man? Who hated oral sex? Who never ever came?

Gone, she thought with a dizzying wave of pleasure. Gone. Gone. Gone.

Her hands lifted to touch the still-burning tips of her breasts before drifting down over her suddenly tense stomach, a shiver running down her spine as she opened her legs once more. Not as wide as before, but wide enough for her hand to slide between her thighs.

'Oh, yes,' she groaned when her fingers brushed over her still-swollen and very sensitive clitoris. She closed her eyes, her hand moving between the slickened folds of flesh till she found the soaked entrance to her body. Never before had she been as wet as this. Or as excited. She moaned at the thought of how it would feel when Sergio filled her there.

Her hand being abruptly pulled away had her eyes flinging open on a startled gasp.

Sergio loomed over her from the side of the bed, his dark gaze glowering with disapproval.

'The only person allowed to touch you there this afternoon is me.'

Bella almost died when he lifted her hand to his mouth and started sucking her fingers, one by one. He seemed to relish the taste of her.

It wasn't till he climbed onto the bed with her again that Bella realised he was now as naked as she was. More naked, actually. She still had her PJ top on, though it was wide open to her waist.

Bella swallowed at the sight of his nakedness. She'd known he was big. She just hadn't anticipated his being that big. Admittedly, he was erect. Stunningly so, his awesome length already housed within a condom. For which Bella was grateful, given her own brains had gone to mush. She *was* on the pill but that didn't protect a woman from all the consequences of unsafe sex.

'Now where were we?' Sergio drawled, his eyes hot on her as he eased her legs further apart and slid his own hand down into her.

Bella sucked in sharply, her heart stopping as his fingertips did things to her insides that made her want to weep with pleasure.

Don't stop, for pity's sake, she groaned silently.

He stopped, which was perhaps just as well, since she'd forgotten to breathe. Her heartbeat lurched back into life as he rolled between her legs and entered her. Just an inch or two at first, but it brought a ragged gasp to her lips.

'Wrap your legs up around my back,' he suggested thickly. 'I don't want to hurt you.'

Hurt her? He wasn't hurting her. He felt fantastic. Already she wanted him in further.

But she did as he asked, and immediately he slid in deeper.

Bella moaned. Oh, God…

Her eyes flung wide when he began to move, her lips falling apart so that she could suck in some much-needed air. But whilst her heart was galloping along at breakneck speed, *his* rhythm was slow and steady. Too slow for her at that moment. And way too steady. She wanted him to ravage her, not make love to her.

'Faster,' she urged him in a voice she barely recognised. 'Faster.'

'I thought you didn't like to talk,' he growled.

When she swore at him he laughed. 'Naughty girl.'

She could not believe it when he withdrew entirely.

She might have sworn at him again but she was distracted by his suddenly flipping her over.

'Let's get you properly naked,' he said, and stripped off her top, leaving her lying there with her back to him and her bottom totally exposed.

And did she care? Not in the slightest. In the past, she would have died a thousand deaths of shame and humiliation. Not so any longer. She loved the feel of Sergio's eyes on her, and his hands on her. And they were.

'So beautiful,' he murmured as he caressed her shoulders then stroked up and down her spine, his finger moving on to tease her still-throbbing clitoris with a skill that had her moaning once more.

When he hoisted her up onto her hands and knees Bella was more than ready to have him take her that way. So she was surprised—and strangely touched—when Sergio asked her if that position was okay by her.

Her 'yes' came out of her mouth in strangled tones, her heart catching in her throat. It was the weirdest moment. She almost felt like crying. But then he was pushing inside her wildly aroused sex and she forgot everything but the feel of his flesh filling hers once more. This time his rhythm wasn't at all slow, his body pounding into her with long, powerful surges. By the time his hands reached round to take rough possession of her breasts she was off in another world, a world where lust reigned supreme. She groaned, her hips wriggling in urgent frustration as she pushed her buttocks back against him, desperate for an end to her erotic torment.

Her climax shook her with the force of an earthquake,

her cries echoing around the marble-floored room, her satisfaction increased by the sound of Sergio's own roar of release, his shuddering as ragged as her own. Finally, Bella collapsed onto the bed, taking Sergio with her. And that was how they lay for simply ages, their chests heaving, their bodies still fused. Gradually, Bella's heartbeat slowed and a languor such as she'd never known before washed through her body, turning all her limbs to liquid. Her last thought before sleep claimed her was that Sergio had been so right. Sex was so much better without the complication of emotion.

CHAPTER TWELVE

SERGIO HEAVED A huge sigh of relief once he realised Bella had fallen fast asleep. For several minutes he just lay there, wallowing in the feel of his sex buried deep inside hers; wallowing in the memory of everything he'd done to her so far. Not nearly enough, of course. He could not wait to have her take him in her mouth. To have her ride him. To make her want him and need him the same way he'd wanted and needed her all these years.

It was a challenging goal, given she was hardly some innocent little virgin who'd never had an orgasm before. How did you enslave a woman with sex when she'd probably already experienced every sexual pleasure and position that existed?

Jeremy had been so wrong when he'd said Bella might not be any good in bed. She'd been great, once she'd got over that silly idea of hers that she had to be in love to enjoy sex. Lord knew where she'd got that idea from, given the kind of mother she had. Darling Dolores hadn't been in love with his father, but she'd still enjoyed sleeping with him. Or so his father had claimed after the divorce, explaining that was why he was so shocked by her announcement that the marriage was over. Sergio realised in hindsight, however, that maybe Dolores was just a good faker.

There'd been nothing fake about Bella's orgasm just now, Sergio's loins leaping anew as he relived the strength of her contractions. The fact that he wanted her again so soon underlined the extent of his desire for her. Though that was hardly a surprise. His desire for Bella had always been obsessive.

Sergio contemplated waking her and having her again. But decided that might not be a good move. Bella was obviously exhausted, not just from the sex. From her busy life and the long flight, plus the ongoing disappointment of men who obviously hadn't loved her the way she'd loved them.

Sergio scowled at this thought. What had it been about those womanising creeps that she'd fallen in love with? Their looks? Their success? Their charm? Possibly all of those things, as well as their bedroom skills. They must have been good lovers. Maybe even great lovers.

Sergio's teeth clenched down hard in his jaw, hating the jab of jealousy that accompanied this last thought. Okay, so she'd been with some major players in the past. So what? He wasn't exactly a novice in bedroom matters. It was crazy to be jealous over Bella's past lovers. Crazy and counterproductive. He should be exploiting her wealth of experience, not getting in a twist about it.

Get your act together, Sergio, and move on.

Very carefully, he slid his half-erect body out of hers and headed for the bathroom, telling himself that those other lovers of hers couldn't have been all that great or she'd have married at least one of them. It seemed impossible that none of them had proposed. Sergio would have liked to ask her what had happened, but feared it was poor form to question a woman over past love affairs. On top of that, giving her the third degree on such matters might reveal more of his own past feelings than he would like.

So keep this affair strictly sexual, Sergio. And don't, you idiot, fall in love with the woman!

The room was dark when Bella finally surfaced, Sergio lying on his back beside her in the bed.

Asleep, thank heavens, giving her time to gather her thoughts before having to make conversation with him. Bella still could not believe how great lovemaking was when you were actually turned on. She shivered with pleasure at the memory of how incredible Sergio had felt, deep inside her. As for that last mind-blowing orgasm… her head had almost exploded when she'd come.

Bella understood now the seductive power of sex, something that had eluded her all these years. She'd always enjoyed being the object of desire, but she'd never actually experienced real desire herself. Till today.

Today had been an eye-opener in more ways than one. It wasn't just her own feelings that had surprised her, but Sergio himself, who'd proved to be nothing like the man she'd always imagined him to be. He was still a gentleman at heart—she could see that. But there was a bad-boy side to him that she found wickedly attractive. It came to her as she lay there, thinking, that she'd always been attracted to bad boys, especially tall, dark and handsome ones. She'd just never lusted after one before. Sergio was a first in that regard.

And what a first!

An erotically charged quiver trickled down Bella's spine as she relived the moment he'd trailed his hand down that same spine, continuing on to where she was happy for him to touch, bringing her quickly back to her earlier level of mindless excitement. Oh, yes, he was a gentleman at heart. Another man might have taken advantage of her at that point; might have pushed her boundaries in a way she was not yet ready for. But not her Sergio.

But he's not *your* Sergio, she reminded herself sternly. Not even remotely. He's just a friend. A friend with benefits. A *temporary* friend with benefits. The only reason he'd suggested such a thing was because he was between girlfriends at the moment. Don't start imagining you're anything special to him.

Bella had no doubt that Sergio had had lots of girlfriends over the years with his dark good looks and impressive body. More than impressive in one department. She glanced over at his nude body, her eyes having adjusted to the darkness by then. She noted that, even at rest, his penis was a full six or seven inches. Erect, he had to be nine at least.

Her mouth dried at the thought of going down on him. But she would manage. Somehow. Because she wanted to. She wanted to very much indeed.

Weird, given she'd always hated doing that. She'd endured it during her earlier relationships. Men did seem to like it a lot. But by the time Andrei had come along, she'd felt confident enough in herself to refuse, saying she simply didn't like doing that. Andrei had been furious with her, accusing her of not loving him. Which of course she hadn't, she realised now. She'd just been infatuated with his larger-than-life persona, then flattered by his dogged pursuit of her.

How good it felt to finally see that she hadn't loved Andrei at all. How liberating. As was her discovery that she could enjoy sex without having to be in love. Though it was a little shocking, in a way. Bella had always been a romantic. Of course, it did make it more acceptable that she liked Sergio. And that he liked her back. She wasn't being wicked at all by indulging in a holiday fling with him.

Well, maybe a little wicked, she thought, giggling as an image came to mind of herself up on her hands and knees, wriggling her bottom in a decidedly wanton fashion.

'That sounded seriously naughty,' Sergio murmured by her side.

'It did, didn't it?' she agreed, resolving not to be coy with him. They were both too adult for coy.

'Dare I ask what you were thinking at the time?' he queried as he rolled over to face her.

'No.'

His dark eyes glittered as his hungry gaze swept over her body, and Bella resisted the momentary urge to cover her nakedness. A bit late to resort to shy. Besides, she liked showing off her body to Sergio; liked the way he looked at it. How amazing was that?

'I could make you tell me,' he threatened. 'I could tickle you till you confess.'

Her eyebrows lifted in a saucy gesture. 'And there I was, thinking you meant to do something seriously naughty to me.'

Now *his* eyebrows lifted. 'You're into seriously naughty, are you?'

Bella realised at that moment that her new boldness was still somewhat shaky. She didn't want Sergio thinking she wanted him to do kinky things.

'Not at all!' she said, trying not to panic.

'What, then?'

'Nothing! I…I was just flirting with you. I didn't have anything specific in mind.'

'You mean you don't want me to tie you to the bedposts and torture you in all sorts of erotic ways till you blurt out all your secret fetishes?'

Bella's eyes blinked wide when the thought of his doing just that sent a wave of dizzying excitement all through her.

'No?' he said, perhaps interpreting her round-eyed gaze as shock. Which was partly true. She was shocked at how much she wanted him to do exactly that. Shocked too that he would suggest such a thing. Clearly, he was even more of a bad boy than she'd realised earlier. Either that, or maybe all men were bad boys when it came to sex. Bella realised she had to take control of the situation—and her own surprisingly lust-filled self—or Sergio might get carried away with what she would allow. She didn't want him believing she was up for anything during her stay here with him.

'No,' she said firmly. 'For your information, dear Sergio, I don't have any secret fetishes. Neither am I into seriously naughty. Now I need to go to the bathroom. And then I need some food.'

'Fair enough,' he said, his nonchalant tone bringing some welcome relief. 'I'll order us a couple of pizzas. You do like pizzas, don't you?' he added with a quirk of his mouth.

Her chin lifted as it did whenever she thought someone was making fun of her.

'I do. If it's a good pizza.'

'Sweetheart, this is Italy. Of course it'll be good pizza.'

Bella flinched at his calling her sweetheart like that. She hated the way men used generic terms for women. She especially hated being called sweetheart and babe. But to take him to task on it seemed petty and premature.

Pursing her lips tightly together, she swung her feet over the side of the bed and was about to stand up when some of her old shyness unexpectedly returned. The thought of walking naked across the room to the bathroom suddenly felt humiliating. She kept picturing him staring at her bare bottom and thinking all sorts of kinky things.

In the end, she squared her shoulders, straightened her spine, stood up and began to slowly cross the marble floor, hotly aware of the way her bottom and hips moved with each step.

His sexy whistle sent a fierce flush to her face. Flustered yet flattered at the same time, she threw what was hopefully a haughty glare over her shoulder at him.

'I'm beginning to think you're no gentleman, after all,' she said.

He just laughed, leaving her no option but to continue on her way whilst valiantly ignoring the memory of the way his eyes were glued to her bottom. And they were, Bella having noted the direction of his gaze when she'd glanced back at him.

But it was no walk of shame in the end. By the time she closed the bathroom door behind her Bella was actually smiling. If felt good to be desired by Sergio. In fact it felt fantastic.

There was a lot to be said for a *friends with benefits* fling, Bella decided. The month ahead promised to be the best holiday she'd ever had, a wonderful combination of the most beautiful setting, wonderfully warm weather and the best sex she'd ever had.

The last bit made her laugh, since she hardly had a history of even *good* sex. If she was brutally honest, her lack of libido over the years had troubled Bella for some time. Had made her feel such a failure in that part of her life. Her lack of sexual confidence was why she'd never been a flirt, only the most persistent admirer getting to first base with her. So why had her libido come to life now? she wondered. And why with Sergio?

All she could think was maybe she was a late bloomer in the sexual sense. She had been late into puberty, never being boy mad as a teenager like other girls. Or maybe it had something to do with Sergio himself. Though what, she couldn't fathom. Yes, he had a great body. And yes, he was also a great lover. But her other boyfriends had all been good-looking men too, as well as very experienced where the ladies were concerned, not to mention way more charming and complimentary in their manner to her. Bella still hadn't forgotten how Sergio had called her too thin. Though he'd also called her beautiful when he'd been making love to her, hadn't he?

'Oh, whatever,' she muttered irritably as she walked over and turned on the taps in the shower.

There really was no point trying to work out such a difficult conundrum. The wonderful reality was that, at last, she'd responded to a man like a normal woman. At last, she'd discovered orgasms. There would be no more boyfriends telling her she was boring in bed. No more believing that she needed to be madly in love to have a satisfying sex life either.

Sergio had shown her that that was a total fallacy, a romantic fantasy. After all, she wasn't in love with him any more than he was in love with her. How liberating was that?

CHAPTER THIRTEEN

'THIS PIZZA IS sinfully yummy,' Bella mumbled with her mouth half full.

'*Sì,*' Sergio replied, and refilled her glass with the bottle of champagne he'd opened in celebration of the way things were going between them.

Her singing in the shower had filled him with a joy that might have troubled him, if it had been any other woman singing in his shower. But this was Bella, the woman who had sexually tormented him for years. And now she was here, in his home and in his bed. Sergio was way too enamoured of her glorious beauty, too bewitched by her sex appeal, too thrilled with having succeeded in her seduction, to dig deeper into his emotions.

They were sitting at a table on the balcony, Bella back in her PJs, Sergio having dragged on a pair of jeans, not needing to play the exhibitionist any longer. She'd already seen what he had to offer. Had experienced it up close and personal. She'd liked it too. Liked it a lot, if he were any judge.

She swallowed, then smiled over at him. 'Do you know that's the first Italian word you've used since I arrived? You've totally lost your accent, do you know that? Not that it was ever strong. Even when you first came to live with us in Sydney, you didn't talk like your father did.'

'That's because I was sent to an English boarding school when I was eight.'

'I vaguely recall you telling me that. Did you like it there?'

'Hated it. I was very happy when our parents married

and my father sent for me to come live with him and go to school in Sydney.' Happy till he'd realised that Dolores didn't really love his father. Or him. Though she'd pretended to. Sergio had always been good at spotting a fake. If it hadn't been for Bella's vivacious company, he would have been miserable. His schooling in Sydney had been barely tolerable, with his never being a popular boy.

'You sounded like a real Aussie for a while,' she said, smiling at the memory. 'Till your dad sent you off to university in Rome and you came back sounding all Italian.'

'Did I? I didn't notice.'

'And now you sound totally English.'

Sergio shrugged. 'Well, I have lived in England for the last eleven years.'

Bella put down the remains of her slice of pizza. 'Doing what, Sergio?'

Before he could think better of it, Sergio started telling her all about his life since their parents' divorce, beginning right back at his first year in Oxford where at last he'd found true male friendship with Alex and Jeremy. He told her all about them, even telling her about their formation of the Bachelors' Club. Admittedly, at the last second, he did have the foresight to let Bella think that their vow to remain bachelors and become billionaires didn't have any age deadline. He wasn't about to give her any inkling that, shortly, he would be looking for a wife.

He then went on to explain how he and his two best friends first got into the wine-bar business, relating that one day, shortly after they'd formed the Bachelors' Club, he and Alex had spotted a dilapidated old bar for sale not far from the Oxford campus. They'd told Jeremy about it that evening, insisting it could be turned into a good business with the right décor and the right wine to appeal to the mainly student clientele. They'd raved about its location, being situated near the university, and they'd known

Jeremy had come into a substantial inheritance from his grandmother's estate, and it wasn't long before they made a deal with him that they would do all the physical work if he put up the money.

'Alex and I did all the refurbishing ourselves,' Sergio told Bella. 'We sanded and varnished the wooden floors and painted all the walls and ceiling black.' He laughed at this memory. 'We'd got a great special from a local paint shop on black paint. Then we hung huge posters of grapes and vineyards on the walls and covered the bar stools in a dark purple vinyl. We got a special on that too. Oh, and we got rid of the mirrors behind the bar. We thought they were too in your face. After that, we hunted the charity shops and flea markets for lounge furniture and coffee tables at reasonable prices and in reasonable condition. We figured our patrons would like somewhere they could relax, or study on their laptops whilst drinking our very affordable wine. The lighting we kept low, mostly with lamps and a few ceiling lights over the bar area. Then we hired the prettiest girls as staff, but dressed them in simple black skirts and white blouses. Nothing too sexy.' He grinned at Bella. 'As I said, they were very pretty girls.'

At this point in his story Sergio realised that Bella was staring at him. No, frowning at him.

'What?' he said.

'But I've been to a wine bar that looks just like that. And it wasn't in Oxford. It was in New York, in a street just off Broadway. It's not far from where I live. It's called Wild Over Wine, but everyone calls it the—'

'WOW bar,' Sergio finished for her. 'Yes. There's a couple of them in New York now.'

Bella's face could not have been more astonished. '*You* own them?'

'No. The Wild Over Wine bars are now a highly successful franchise. After the success of our first bar, we bought another, then another. Always near a university at first, but in the end anywhere which had a good location. Eventually, things got too much for us to handle, despite Jeremy having finally come on board as our chief financial officer. Anyway, I got this bright idea to start up a franchise. And it took off. Soon there were WOW bars all over Great Britain and even some in Australia and New Zealand, thanks to Alex. I did tell you Alex was Australian, didn't I?'

Bella nodded.

'Brilliant salesman. Brilliant all round, actually. Anyway, recently the franchise started creeping into America, with considerable success, I might add.'

'I can imagine. I loved the one I went into. It had a highly individual ambience with its black walls and comfy furniture. But I wouldn't have said the wine was all that cheap.'

'Yes, well, we did change our ideas on that in the end. You can still buy cheap wine at WOW bars if that's all you can afford, but we were forced to also cater for well-heeled clients whose palates required something better. Oh, and we changed the background music to classical. No royalty paying on most classical music,' he added laughingly.

'Heavens!' Bella exclaimed. 'I would never have guessed you would become a successful businessman. I always imagined you as some kind of academic.'

Sergio tried not to be offended. He *had* been a bit of a nerd as a teenager, always with his head in a book.

'Well, I was never unsure of *your* career path,' he pointed out. 'From the time you were just a kid you were destined for fame and fortune in the music world. All your many and various successes have never surprised me.'

She actually looked a little embarrassed by his compliments.

'That's sweet of you to say so, Sergio, but, to be honest, fame and fortune isn't all it's cracked up to be. When

I'm doing a musical on stage, I work terribly long hours. It can be exhausting, and, quite frankly, rather lonely. I don't always have time for a social life, or proper relationships.' She sighed a sigh that carried a wealth of irony, her blue eyes darkening as she picked up her champagne and took a deep swallow. 'I know you probably think I've had heaps of affairs. But that's far from the truth. In the last decade I've only had three serious relationships, all with men best forgotten.'

Sergio didn't know what to say, her revelation bringing a mixture of surprise and scepticism. Which were the three? The French actor had to be one. And definitely that Russian fellow. Which left a toss-up between the Brazilian polo player and the American rock star. If she was to be believed, that was. Yet why would she lie to him? What motive could she possibly have?

'I did read about your dating Chuck Richards at one stage,' he said at last, trying to sound offhand and not accusatory.

'Good God, no. I never dated that creep. Unfortunately, my publicist at the time thought it was good for my career for my name to be connected in the media with high-profile celebrities. At the time Chuck was all the rage. I was talked into accompanying him to the Aria awards that year, oblivious of the fact that he was a cocaine addict. I had to fight him off in the limo all the way back to my hotel. The guy was an octopus. I told him what I thought of him when I could finally get out, but of course it was reported in the papers as a lovers' spat. Something Chuck didn't deny. He made it sound like we'd been secretly seeing each other for weeks. I fired that publicist, but the next one I hired wasn't much better.'

'Why have one, then?' Sergio asked.

Bella shrugged. 'It's the way the world works in America. You aren't anyone in show business if you don't have a manager and a publicist and a stylist. I even have a Hollywood agent.'

'You're going into movies next?' Was she mad? She was already suffering from burnout.

'Maybe. If the right movie comes along.'

'It's a mistake to have too many fingers in too many pies, Bella,' Sergio advised, feeling genuinely worried for her. 'I found that out myself this last year. With my father gone, I felt I should come back to Milan to try to rescue the family business, which was close to bankruptcy. Not out of some silly male pride, but because lots of families rely on that business for their living. Times are just as tough economically in Italy as they are all over the world. Anyway, I knew I couldn't do that and manage the franchise as well. One of them had to go. I couldn't do both.'

'So what did you do?'

'I talked it over with Alex and Jeremy and, with their approval, I sold the franchise, along with the wine bars we actually owned.'

'I hope you got a good price.'

He grinned. 'Let's just say the main goal of the Bachelors' Club was instantly achieved.'

'You all became billionaires?'

'We did indeed.' No point in hiding the fact. After all, he didn't need to use money as a lever to seduce her. She was already well and truly seduced.

'But that's marvellous! Oh, you are a clever boy. Now all you have to do is save the family business.'

'Yes,' he said, doing his best not to look smug. 'Unfortunately, that's going to be a tall order. But I'll give it my best shot.'

'I'm sure you will. So you're going to be living here in future?'

'Only at weekends. The family owns a town house in Milan where I'll stay during the week.'

'I see.' She took the last bite of her pizza, her expression thoughtful. 'You say family, Sergio, but there's only you now. Hardly a family. Don't you want to get married and have children one day? Surely you don't intend to stay a bachelor for ever!'

Sergio could see that he'd backed himself into a corner with his earlier lie. But he really didn't want her to know about his plan to look for a wife soon. It would make their affair seem...callous. Which, of course, it was.

Any guilt he felt was quickly dismissed, however. Why should he feel guilty? She was having a good time, wasn't she? And he was getting what he'd always wanted.

'I'm rather obsessive when I am faced with a challenge,' he confessed. 'I won't have time for a wife and children till the family business is making a profit, which could take years. Besides, I'm only thirty-four. I have plenty of time yet to get married.'

Bella pulled a face. 'Wish I could say the same. Women don't have all the time in the world if they want children. I turned thirty last month. My biological clock is ticking.'

Sergio suppressed the crazy urge to suggest he would give her a child, if she desperately wanted one. 'Come now, Bella,' he said, 'from the sounds of things you hardly have time to have sex, let alone children.'

'True,' she said, then laughed, her eyes sparkling as she looked over the table at him. 'Till today, that is. I still can't believe how great it was between us. I mean...it was amazing!'

Sergio could not believe how swiftly his mind switched from having a simple chat with Bella to wanting to have sex with her again, his desire as strong as ever. He'd been right in his original assessment that it would take at least a month of having her before he could move on with his life. She was like a disease, one that he had no antibiotics for. Only time would make him immune to this power she had over him.

Thankfully, she didn't know she possessed such power; didn't know how much he wanted her.

He was just a friend with benefits.

'I agree,' he said. 'So now that you've had some decent food, do you fancy trying another of Mother Nature's sleeping pills?'

Her eyes rounded a little but he could see she was as eager as he was. 'You're not too tired?' she asked.

He had to smile. 'Not yet,' he said, then swallowed the last of his wine. She had no idea, did she? Which was exactly what he wanted. 'Shall we try your room this time?' he suggested casually. 'That way you won't have to answer any awkward questions when Maria finds your bed unused tomorrow.'

'Oh, God,' she said, perplexing him with a sudden blush. 'I'd forgotten about what Maria might think.'

Sergio shook his head at her. Women, he'd found over the years, were often complex, contradictory creatures. They often said one thing and meant another. He didn't want to even try to understand Bella at this moment. He just wanted to have sex with her. Over and over and over.

'Let me worry about Maria,' he said as he stood up and held out his hand towards her. 'All you have to do tonight is enjoy the benefits of our friendship.'

He loved the way her eyes dilated as she put her hand in his; loved the evidence of her own desire. This time, he thought rather ruthlessly as he drew her to her feet, he would insist she be on top, but only after she'd pleasured him with that luscious mouth of hers. Tonight, he wanted to watch her face as she came; wanted to feel her coming apart whilst he was buried deep inside her; wanted to witness her totally losing control.

Only then would he let himself go. Only then.

CHAPTER FOURTEEN

BELLA SOMEHOW GOT her legs to carry her into the cream and gold bedroom where Sergio finally dropped her hand from his. Not that this afforded her much relief, since he immediately started to undo the buttons on her top. Her body swayed slightly as her mind reeled. She wanted him even more desperately this time. Wanted him so much that she felt almost ill. Her heart was racing and her stomach churning. She was tempted to reach up and rip the top off herself, so impatient was she to be naked before him. When he finally peeled the top back off her shoulders, her belly tightened alarmingly, making her fiercely aware of her full bladder. Too much of that champagne, she realised with some dismay.

'I...I need to go to the bathroom,' she said shakily.

His dark eyes narrowed. 'You're not going cold on me, are you?' he asked.

'God, no,' she choked out. She was so hot she was on the verge of combustion!

'Come back naked, then. I like my women naked.'

Bella sucked in sharply at the sudden harshness in his voice, and in his statement.

He seemed to sense her hurt for he immediately reached out to run a softly seductive finger down her cheek and around her mouth. 'But only when they're as lovely as you, beautiful Bella,' he murmured.

Her chin still lifted, her pride stung by being lumped together with all his other women. And there would have been plenty. She could see that. Perversely, she didn't like that thought. 'I would imagine you don't go to bed with any other kind,' she snapped, stupidly letting her jealousy show.

He smiled a knowing smile, his provocative finger dropping away. 'You could be right. But it's a common failing in bachelors. And beautiful women. I can't see you going to bed with an ugly man.'

She could not find an answer to that. Despite their flaws, her lovers had all been tall, dark and handsome. Like Sergio. But there'd only been three of them whereas she suspected he'd had girlfriends galore. Who would have guessed that the reserved boy she'd come to know and like enormously would one day become a playboy? And a billionaire as well!

'Let's not have a lovers' tiff,' he went on, still smiling. 'Now go do what you have to do. I need to get some condoms from my room, anyway. We'll meet back on this bed *sans* clothes in a couple of minutes, okay?'

Bella tried to hold on to her resentment at his high-handed attitude but it was futile. Already she was a slave to the exquisite pleasure that going to bed with Sergio promised. As much as she didn't like the idea of his being a playboy, his wealth of experience did have some compensations. He certainly knew what he was doing in bed. Which was more than could be said for her. But she was learning.

It did cross Bella's mind that her past lovers had all been playboys as well, with lots of bedroom experience. But she'd never had an orgasm with them. Never wanted them the way she wanted Sergio. It was a puzzle all right, she thought as she stripped off her clothes and stared at herself in the large vanity mirror, taking in her pink cheeks and erect nipples. But not a puzzle she cared to think about for long. All she wanted was to get back out there and be waiting for Sergio, naked, the way he liked his women.

He was there before her, stretched out on top of the

cream cotton sheets, as naked as she was. More naked this time, she noted, no condom covering the awesome length of his erection.

When she stared, then hesitated to join him on the bed, Sergio rolled over onto his side and pointed to the pile of condoms sitting on the bedside table right next to her. 'I will use one when it's strictly necessary,' he told her. 'But till then, I thought it might be more pleasurable without protection.'

Bella found his casual manner exasperating yet perversely exciting. Could it be that his taking all the emotion out of the situation made her relax and actually enjoy the sex? It seemed a possible solution to the puzzle. Certainly, when she was with Sergio, she wasn't wondering if he really loved her or not. Because she knew he didn't!

Shaking her head at him, she climbed onto the bed, determined to act as casually as he was. But it was just an act. Suddenly, her earlier eagerness to take him in her mouth faded in the face of actually doing it. Her mouth dried at the thought.

Time for some of that new boldness, Bella. Time to take the reins, perhaps. Something you're not used to doing, but you're not an idiot, or ignorant. You know what men like.

'Right,' she said briskly. 'Just lie back, Sergio, and I'll see if I can help you out with your sleeping problem.'

Oddly enough, her deciding to take control of the situation did wonders for her own sudden lack of confidence. As she sat up and bent her head towards Sergio's impatient flesh, Bella experienced the same rush of adrenalin that always swept through her once she actually stepped out onto a stage and began to sing. Performing for an audience always thrilled her. She was never nervous at all, not once the show actually started. Of course, it did help that she always practised her role and her songs till she was note perfect.

The role she was about to play was not one she'd overly practised, or even remotely perfected.

She should have experienced a crisis of confidence but she didn't.

I can do this, she told herself as her lips hovered above him. I am a quick study. And observant. I will soon know what pleases him most.

Bella sucked in a deep breath, her lips falling apart in a last moment of panic.

CHAPTER FIFTEEN

SERGIO SHUDDERED WHEN her lips brushed over the straining tip of his erection.

Dear God, what an idiot am I to think I could stand this for more than a few seconds.

His teeth clenched down hard in his jaw when she did it again, his gut tightening as he braced himself for more torment. And she gave him more, doing everything that he'd ever dreamt of her doing. Licking him. Kissing him. Sucking him. Then taking him into her mouth, slowly, inch by inch, till he couldn't bear it any more.

'No,' he grunted out when he was right on the verge of coming.

Her head immediately lifted, her eyes glazed, her lips looking swollen yet soft and luscious and deliciously wet.

'No?' she queried, sounding totally confused. And of course she would be. The men she'd been with would have let her go all the way; would have demanded it. But that was not what *he* wanted. Not this time. He wanted to come inside her. Wanted her to make love to him with her whole body, not just her mouth.

'No,' he repeated, his voice rough and raw. 'That's enough of that. I want the real thing, after all.'

She didn't say a word, just stared down at him for a long moment. But then she gave herself a little shake of her shoulders and reached for a condom.

'I think you'd better put this on,' she said, her hand trembling in a way that almost got to him.

So she was turned on to the max. That was good, wasn't it? It didn't mean anything special.

He tore the packet open with his teeth and sheathed himself without a fumble.

'What's so funny?' he said when he noticed her small smile.

'Just thinking how practice makes perfect.'

He almost retorted that he'd been thinking exactly the same thing about her. But he had enough common sense left to know how easily women could be put off by the wrong comment.

So he just smiled and rolled over on top of her, his erection pressed between them.

'I want to kiss that delicious mouth of yours whilst it still tastes of me.'

His mouth hovered over hers. 'You are seriously sexy. Now kiss me, Bella.'

A wave of dark triumph rushed through him when she obeyed him. Though she did close her eyes, as if by doing that she was lessening his power over her. But it only strengthened his resolve to seduce her further, to make her do things that perhaps she hadn't done before, make her want him to dominate her totally.

He sent his tongue in deep before setting up a rhythm that echoed what he ached to do to her. In and out, in and out, till she was gasping for breath. Only then did he stop, withdrawing totally, then rolling over onto his back, taking her with him.

'Sit up, Bella,' he commanded, and she did so, staring dazedly down at him as she sat up and straddled him.

'Now take down your hair.'

God, but he adored the way her hands shook as they lifted to do his bidding. Seeing her so turned on didn't make up for all the years he'd suffered because of his unrequited passion for her, but it was something.

He watched in awe as her glorious hair tumbled in erotic disarray around her shoulders. It was her crowning glory, her hair; soft and silky with a slight wave when dry and lots of curls when wet. He glanced down at where only the narrowest strip of fair curls guarded her sex. Some chose to totally denude their bodies but he'd always preferred a little mystery.

Bella still remained a mystery to him in some ways. But not in the bedroom. She obviously liked being in control sometimes. But mostly she preferred playing the submissive role. That was fine by him. He liked being the boss in the bedroom.

'You can take over now,' he said, appealing to both sides of her nature.

She looked startled for a split second, but then smiled, a rather enigmatic smile that he could not read. Without saying a word, she rose up onto her knees, her eyes dropping to his freed erection. A groan hovered on his lips when she grasped it with both hands, directing it carefully but inexorably to the entrance to her body. Both their eyes remained glued to that spot, Sergio's heartbeat ceasing as his flesh began to slowly disappear within hers.

Dear God…it felt incredible. *She* was incredible. And so hot.

He didn't start breathing again till he was fully inside her. He might have stayed relatively sane if she hadn't started to move, rising up high then sinking back down upon him with her eyes shut, her head thrown back in an attitude of blissful rapture. Her own breathing grew more rapid, a harsh panting escaping from her parted lips. She was off in another world, a world where it didn't seem to matter what male body was underneath her. And did he care? Hell, no. He was too far gone to care about anything but being released from the agony that was gripping his sex.

Her first contraction sent him over the edge, his hips jerking up from the bed as he ejaculated into her with the violence of an erupting volcano. Reaching blindly for her shoulders, he dragged her down on top of him, holding her tightly whilst their bodies throbbed and shuddered together, wallowing in the fact that she was as crazy in lust as he was.

If only she hadn't nestled into his neck with her face. If only she hadn't pressed her mouth against his skin, murmuring his name at the same time.

His heart immediately squeezed tight, then flowered open, emotion flooding in.

His groan was the groan of defeat. Or was it resignation?

He could keep telling himself it was just lust dictating his actions with Bella; and this was true to a degree. But Sergio could no longer pretend that his emotions hadn't become involved as well. Was it love yet? He hoped not. He'd never actually fallen in love before so he had nothing to guide him. But he could not deny that she was getting under his skin in more ways than just sexual. Which was most unfortunate. Bella didn't *want* him to fall in love with her, and he sure as hell didn't want to fall in love with her. Once their holiday fling was over, she would return to her life on the other side of the world, with this interlude just a pleasant memory. Their friendship—even with benefits—would not survive. She'd get sucked back into her career and that would be that. She wouldn't give him a second thought, the way she hadn't when their parents had divorced all those years ago. It had been bad enough lusting after her from afar. He didn't want to love her from afar as well.

Sergio decided then and there to make sure that didn't happen.

So get your butt out of this bed, Sergio, he told himself

firmly. And cut back on the sex from now on. She's too damned good at it, that's the trouble. All these fabulous climaxes are scrambling your brains, and messing with your emotions. The plan to get her out of your system was seriously flawed from the start. Logic should have told you that once you had Bella in your bed, you'd be in danger of becoming even more obsessed with her.

It took a supreme effort of will for Sergio to extricate himself from under her body, especially when she moaned and tried to cling to him. Thankfully, her limbs were weak, though her eyelids fluttered open when he pulled the sheet up over her.

'Don't leave me,' she begged softly.

God, but she was the very devil; a siren calling him to sure disaster.

He had to get out of here. And now!

'Go to sleep, Bella,' he commanded. 'You've had enough for tonight. And quite frankly, so have I.'

So saying, he whirled round and strode from the bedroom before she could glimpse that he *hadn't* had enough of her. Not by a long shot!

His self-lecturing didn't stop after he returned to the master bedroom, continuing all through the long cold shower he forced himself to endure.

'No sex tomorrow,' Sergio muttered as the icy shards of water lashed his burgeoning erection into retreat. 'Thankfully, Maria will be here for a few hours during the day. That should stop me from going skinny dipping with Bella in the pool, then sweeping her off to the master bedroom for a lazy afternoon of non-stop lovemaking.'

Unfortunately, both ideas projected arousing images that refused to be banished. Sergio imagined their indulging in lots of oral foreplay in the pool and its surrounds. Maybe he'd even let her go all the way with that delicious mouth of hers. God, but she was good at that. Once he came that way, he'd be able to take his time with her in bed without his own frustration getting the better of him. He could play with her for ages. Maybe even bind her to the bedposts. Would she let him do that? he wondered. Possibly not yet. But soon, she would. He was sure of it. She—

Sergio abruptly pulled himself up short. What in hell did he think he was doing, making plans for seducing Bella further? He was supposed to be working out how to reduce the amount of sex between them, not increase it.

He shook his head at himself, vowing to do everything in his power to take control of the situation. Some sex with Bella was fine. But only last thing at night, and only under the pretext of helping them both with their insomnia. Because let's face it, Sergio, you're not going to be able to sleep till you've had her again. But sex during the day is simply not on. That will only lead to your becoming addicted to her. Or worse!

By the time Sergio emerged from the shower, he had his body and his mind under control. He also had a plan to survive the next month, because that was what it had come down to. Surviving. Of course, having a plan and putting it into action were sometimes two different things entirely. It also wouldn't help that he would have Maria playing matchmaker the whole time Bella was here. Thank God he'd accepted that invitation to go to dinner at Claudia's tomorrow night. That would take care of a few hours in the evening when temptation would be at its highest. And thank God come Monday he could legitimately spend every weekday at the factory in Milan. If truth be told, it was high time he got to work with sorting out the family business, anyway. Maybe, if he got deeply involved with that, being with Bella would lessen in importance.

And maybe the sun won't come up tomorrow, Sergio, he thought with a rueful laugh.

He sighed a deep sigh and ordered himself to go to bed

and go to sleep. Unfortunately, he wasn't as good at obeying his orders as Bella. Sergio tossed and turned for ages, not dropping off till the sky was turning that peculiar shade of mauve that preceded the dawn. When he eventually regained consciousness, the balcony outside the master bedroom was bathed in sunshine.

The sun *had* come up, was his first thought.

CHAPTER SIXTEEN

THE KITCHEN IN the villa was large and welcoming, with a flagstone floor, pine cupboards, marble benchtops and a central wooden table that could seat up to eight people. When Bella entered it shortly after noon Sergio was seated at the far end of the table, dressed in colourful board shorts and a white T-shirt. His eyes were down, his large hands cupped around a steaming mug of what she presumed was coffee. He still hadn't shaved and he looked even sexier to Bella than he had yesterday. Maria was standing at the kitchen sink, humming away and staring through the window at the lake beyond.

Sergio's head lifted at her arrival, his dark gaze sweeping over her from top to toe before returning to her face, a small smile curving that wicked mouth of his.

It was a struggle not to look embarrassed in any way. But she managed, Bella having determined before coming downstairs not to act like some simpering virgin whom Sergio had seduced against her will. When she'd first woken this morning, the memories of the day before had momentarily overwhelmed her. In a way, it all seemed surreal. Her unexpected lust for Sergio. His astonishing proposal that they have a *friends with benefits* fling. And then her even more astonishing boldness in bed.

Was that really her, going down on him so avidly, then sitting on top of him and riding him so wildly and wantonly?

Part of her had wanted to shrink from that person. Her

mother had brought her up to believe that nice girls definitely didn't do things like that.

Thinking about her mother's hypocritical advice over the years had quickly banished any sense of shame over the night before, Bella accepting with a new sexual maturity that she'd enjoyed every incredibly exciting second. She'd especially enjoyed experiencing her first orgasms. Lord, but she'd never dreamt of such pleasure. Or such blissful satisfaction.

Bella wondered momentarily as she smiled at Sergio how he would react if she told him she'd never had an orgasm before last night?

Not that she would. He clearly believed she was an experienced woman of the world. To reveal that the opposite was the case might send him running a mile, something she certainly didn't want. What Bella wanted more than anything was more of what she'd had last night. She actually found amusement in the realisation that her mother would *die* at the R-rated desires running through her darling daughter's head.

'Good morning,' she said brightly as she pulled out the chair at the opposite end of the table.

Maria immediately spun around from the sink.

'At last! Someone is up who will eat breakfast!' she exclaimed. 'Sergio, he just want coffee. But not decent Italian coffee. He prefer that weak rubbish they drink in London. So what you want, Bella? A nice omelette, perhaps? But first a cup of espresso.'

Bella looked sheepish as she sat down. 'Would you be offended if I had what Sergio's having?'

Sergio laughed. 'See, Maria? I am not the only one with a weak stomach this morning.'

'Pah! You two. I know why you no want breakfast. Too much pizza and champagne last night.'

'Too much something,' Sergio muttered under his

breath, then smiled at Bella, his eyes glittering with a knowing amusement.

Bella kept her cool on the outside, but her insides didn't fare quite so well. Truly, the man was the devil in disguise. Who would have believed that the once-conservative Sergio would turn into such a Casanova?

Not that she really minded.

'So how did you sleep?' he asked her.

'Very well,' she replied without batting an eyelid. 'And you?'

'Like a log.'

'Champagne always makes me drowsy,' she said, determined to play the game as well as he did.

'Then we'll open another bottle tonight.'

'I thought you were going to your neighbour's place for dinner tonight,' she reminded him.

'So I am. But I shouldn't get back too late.'

'I might have gone to bed by then.'

He shrugged. 'There's always another night.'

It irked Bella that he wasn't as keen to be with her again as she was to be with him. But then why would he be? Last night hadn't been anything special to him. Not as it had been for her.

Maria scowled as she placed a mug of coffee down in front of Bella. 'I do not come here just to make rubbish coffee.' She placed her hands on her wide hips and glowered at them.

'I know!' she exclaimed, suddenly beaming. 'I will pack you both a picnic basket. Sergio, you will take Bella out in the rowing boat. Go to that secret cove you found when fishing a while ago. That way, Bella does not have to wear any silly wig. She can be herself.'

Bella's stomach flipped over at the thought of going on a romantic picnic lunch with Sergio in some secret cove.

He didn't seem quite as keen on the idea, however, if his expression was anything to go by.

'I don't know about that,' he said. 'It's always very busy on the lake on a Sunday. Someone in a passing boat might recognise Bella.'

'Not if I wear dark glasses and a large hat,' she said straight away, locking eyes with his.

His scowl was more than a match for Maria's. 'Be it on your head, then. But I suggest you wear something different from that,' he added, nodding at the white cheesecloth skirt and shirt she had on. 'The top is okay. But you'll need a swimming costume under it. It's hot today and the water in the cove is perfect for swimming.'

Bella's stomach tightened when she thought of the brief white bikini she'd bought at the airport. She hadn't bought it with seduction in mind but it had seduction written all over it.

'Fine,' she said, doing her best to look innocent.

His dark eyes narrowed slightly.

'Maria, how long will it take to put that picnic basket together?' he asked.

'Not long. Ten, fifteen minutes.'

'I'll go get the boat out. Bella, you go put that swimming costume on. And don't bother with make-up. You don't need it, anyway.'

Bella decided to take that as a compliment, despite his brusque tone. Sergio might be Casanova in bed at night but super charming in the daytime, he wasn't.

'Can I finish my coffee first?' she asked.

'If you must.'

'I must. Then I have to go to the toilet and put my swimming costume on.'

He rolled his eyes. 'And how long will that take?'

She shrugged. 'Fifteen minutes. Tops.' You learned to be quick when you worked on stage.

Sergio gave her a droll look as he stood up. 'I'll believe that when I see it. Women don't know the meaning of punctuality. Just try not to keep me waiting too long.' And he stalked off.

'He's a bit grumpy in the morning, isn't he?' Bella said as she finished her coffee.

Maria sighed. 'Sergio. He has been sad since his papa passed away. But he will be better now that he come home to Italy to live. Even better when he finds himself a wife. Maybe someone nice like you, Bella. It is time you got married, is it not?'

Though somewhat startled by Maria's unexpected suggestion, Bella could not help wallowing in the romantic fantasy of marrying Sergio for a few silly seconds. Till common sense kicked back in. No way would Sergio ever ask her to marry him. Frankly, she was amazed that he'd forgiven her enough to be her friend. Though of course that friendship now came with benefits, benefits that she'd enjoyed last night as much as him. Hopefully, she would enjoy some more of those benefits during their romantic picnic by the lake; just the thought of being with Sergio again made her head spin and her heart race.

'Sergio isn't interested in getting married just yet, Maria,' she said, jumping up from the table and carrying the mug over to the sink. 'And neither am I.' Her interests lay elsewhere at the moment. 'Now I'd better hurry.'

Seventeen minutes later she was sitting in the back of a rather ancient-looking wooden rowing boat whilst casting an envious glance at the gleaming red and white speedboat still sitting in the boat shed. The picnic basket was safely stowed under her seat, Sergio using a battered oar to push the boat away from the shore. He hadn't changed his clothes, though he was now wearing sunglasses. Understandable, given the brightness of the day. And the water.

'I think I should warn you,' she said with slightly feigned nonchalance, 'that Maria is trying to matchmake us.'

His expression showed this was not news to him, which perhaps explained his irritable mood. Maybe Maria had said something to him this morning before she'd come downstairs.

'Maria is a romantic,' he said with an exasperated shrug of his broad shoulders.

'Most women are romantics at heart,' Bella confessed. Herself included. Only a romantic would ever have imagined that one day she would find a man who would love her as deeply as she loved him; who would understand her and support her; who would be a great father as well as a fabulous husband. Such thinking was the stuff fantasies were made of. Fantasies and Hollywood movies.

Bella actually thought it sweet of Maria to imagine that she would make Sergio a good wife. Because of course she wouldn't. Their sex life might be fine but that was about it.

Her sigh carried a degree of regret that life was infinitely more complicated for a woman once she had a successful career, especially one that was as essential to her as breathing. Bella might be suffering from burnout at the moment, but she could never give up performing. Singing for an audience made her soul soar in ways she could never describe. Without it, she would be a mere shadow of herself.

'What did she say to you?' Sergio asked as he began to row.

His impatient tone made Bella worry that she might have got Maria into trouble.

'Oh, nothing much. Just that I would make you a good wife. Which was rather amusing. I can't imagine a less suitable wife for you. Anyway, I told Maria neither of us wanted marriage at the moment. I hope you don't mind my speaking for you.'

'Not at all. I appreciate it.'

Just then a couple of jet skis zoomed past them, their wakes causing the rowing boat to rock back and forth, Bella sucking in sharply as she clung to the sides.

Sergio swore at them before apologising to Bella for his language. 'Lake Como in the tourist season is not what it used to be,' he told her.

'Yes, I can see that,' Bella said with regret in her voice. 'But I suppose you can't blame people for coming here. It's such a beautiful place, especially in the summer.'

'I blame the authorities for allowing cowboys like that to spoil other people's pleasure. This is a place to relax. It is not a speedway.'

'Yet *you* have a speedboat,' she pointed out mischievously.

'I do not drive it like a cowboy.'

She laughed. 'I'll believe that when I see it. Now where is this cove you're taking me to?'

'It's a little way yet. If we stop talking I will row faster. Just admire the scenery and relax.'

Bella stopped talking but she didn't relax. Perhaps because the scenery she started admiring had nothing to do with her beautiful surrounds but the man right in front of her eyes, his action of rowing focusing her attention on his magnificent physique and the way the biceps in his arms bulged with each stroke. It was to be thanked that she was wearing sunglasses because they let her ogle him shamelessly without being obvious. The instant and intense desire she'd felt for him yesterday by the pool returned with a rush, making her belly tighten and her nipples tingle. She could not wait to reach the privacy of this cove, the word *secret* suggesting that they would be unobserved there. They would be all alone…

Sergio could *feel* her eyes on him.

Yet he wasn't even looking at her. He dared not. To look

upon her exquisite beauty was sheer torture for him. The
hat and the sunglasses didn't help at all. He could still see
her body, which was covered ineffectually by a semi-sheer
white shirt and what looked like a very skimpy white bikini underneath. And then there were her legs...her very
long, very bare legs. God, but her legs were something
else. A dancer's legs. Well toned yet graceful with slender
ankles and shapely calves and lovely firm thighs, thighs
that he started imagining wrapped around him whilst he...

Gritting his teeth, Sergio dragged his mind back from
the brink of hell, kept his eyes down and concentrated on
the rhythm of his rowing stroke. He was a good rower.
He'd rowed at Oxford, his team of eight winning the re-
gatta one year. Alex had been in the same team, but not
Jeremy, who'd broken his leg skiing. He'd had to be content cheering from the banks of the river. Which he'd done
very well in the company of his girlfriend at the time, as
well as all the girlfriends of the rest of the team.

Sergio smiled at the memory. He was a devil with the
ladies, was Jeremy.

'What are you smiling at?' Bella asked, forcing Sergio
to glance up at her.

'I was thinking of my rowing days at Oxford.'

'It was a rather wicked smile,' she pointed out with a
knowing smile of her own.

'I was also thinking of my friend, Jeremy.'

'What about him?'

'Jeremy was the resident Don Juan of the university.'

'Isn't that the pot calling the kettle black?'

Sergio laughed. 'Hardly. No man alive could keep up
with Jeremy when it comes to the game of musical beds.
He's now a grand master.'

'Being a Don Juan is hardly an admirable trait.'

'You don't know Jeremy. There's no malice in him. All
his exes still hold him in high regard.'

'So you don't consider yourself a Don Juan?'

'Not at all. I did sow some wild oats when I was at Oxford but since then my sex life has been on the conservative side. Just one girlfriend at a time.'

'I see. And how long does a girlfriend usually last?'

'A lot longer than Jeremy's,' he said drily. 'Though I must confess I've had a few over the years.'

'And you've never fallen in love?'

Sergio realised this conversation was getting too close to the bone. He'd also almost rowed right past the cove.

'Not even close,' he said abruptly. 'Now, if you don't mind stopping with the twenty questions, we're here. And this next part is a little tricky to negotiate.'

Bella had been grateful for the distraction of talking. She'd also been genuinely interested in finding out more about Sergio, the man. But once silence fell between them, she was catapulted back to her earlier state where her longing to be with him again overwhelmed all other emotions. Suppressing a sigh, she glanced around her, frowning as she realised that her mental picture of Sergio's secret cove bore little resemblance to reality. There was no cute little beach with soft sand. Just a U-shaped inlet, the shoreline bordered by an ancient stone wall as was common around the lake. The wall was quite high; Bella not seeing herself clambering up over it from a rocking boat. Neither could she see herself swimming in the water, which looked cold and deep, not at all warm. Where they would have a picnic she had no idea, unless it was in the boat.

'The water line is higher than when I was last here,' Sergio said as he angled the boat round a slight bend, Bella relieved to see a set of well-worn steps carved into the wall. There was also a large iron ring bolted into the wall to which Sergio secured the boat.

'Don't worry,' he said when he saw her frowning.

'There's a lovely little secret garden on the other side of the wall. But I don't think we'll be going swimming. Best leave that till we get back to the villa.'

He hadn't exaggerated. There was a truly delightful secret garden on the other side of the wall, with soft mossy grass underneath shady pine trees and an abundance of flowering shrubs exuding a variety of scents. It was obvious, however, that the garden hadn't been tended for some time. There was no villa nearby, that she could see. Not that she could see very far; the bushes and trees were too thick.

'Are we trespassing on private property?' she asked as Sergio placed the wicker picnic basket under a shady tree then reached for the checked blanket resting on the double-handled lid.

'Possibly,' he confessed as he spread the blanket out on the ground. 'But we're not doing any harm. Clearly, no one uses this place any more. Come on, I don't know about you but I'm suddenly starving.'

Bella had to agree once he opened the basket and she saw what Maria had packed for them. And there she'd been, thinking her hunger was only for Sergio. She swiftly knelt down to help him unpack all the goodies, her mouth watering over the simple but yummy-looking food. Along with two baguettes of freshly baked bread, there was a delicious selection of cold meat and cheeses, two huge bunches of fat juicy grapes, plus a couple of sinfully fattening pastries. No wine, just a flask full of iced coffee, along with two unbreakable glasses.

By the time Bella had devoured more than her fair share, all she wanted to do was lie back on that blanket and go to sleep. Her sigh of contentment echoed against the wall as she stretched out and closed her eyes.

'I take it you won't be needing me this time to help you sleep?'

Bella's eyelids fluttered upwards to find him lying on his side, watching her with smouldering eyes.

Her desire for him was instant, her drowsiness of a moment ago gone like a flash.

What to say? Bella still wasn't totally used to this new lustful creature who'd emerged to take control of her life, and who could tempt her with the wickedest of urges.

She wanted to lie naked with him on this blanket. She wanted him on top of her this time. On top of her and inside her. Filling her, and confounding her. Taking her with him again to that place where she didn't think, or worry, or care; where all she wanted was to wallow in the most incredible physical pleasure, followed by the most brilliant of releases.

Heat flooded her face as she sat up and started undoing the buttons on her top. He didn't move, his gaze fixed on her as she undressed. At last she was totally naked, her clothes neatly folded on the grass, topped by her hat and sunglasses. She didn't say a word, just lay back on the blanket and looked at him.

CHAPTER SEVENTEEN

SERGIO REALISED RIGHT then and there that his vow to cut back on the sex was almost impossible to keep, especially with Bella lying naked and willing in front of him. Admittedly, he'd been asking for trouble with that leading question about her needing his help to sleep. But he'd never expected her to do what she'd just done.

The exquisite beauty of her naked body was a powerful aphrodisiac, but the naked desire in her eyes was even more powerful. No man could resist the way she was obviously wanting him. Sergio certainly couldn't.

To give himself credit, he did try, using the age-old excuse that he hadn't brought any condoms with him.

She blinked at him, then smiled. 'It's okay,' she said, her voice all soft and smoky. 'I'm on the pill. And before you ask,' she added, 'after I broke up with Andrei I had every test known to mankind. All came back negative, thank God.'

Sergio didn't need any further encouragement. Neither did he give her any reassurances about his own clean bill of health. Though he could have. Possibly should have. But he was already kissing her, kissing her and touching her, pushing her legs apart and losing himself in the hot, wet silkiness that awaited him there. Her moans brought him to the brink with a speed that forced him to abandon her for a few seconds so that he could strip off his own clothes. No way was he going to come without being inside her.

She gasped when he entered her, then groaned, her legs lifting to wrap around him, the action giving him room to slide in deeper. God, but she felt incredible, her muscles tight around him. He didn't dare move too vigorously, knowing that he would come within seconds. So he started rocking back and forth slowly with his hips, bracing himself above her on his elbows to keep contact to a minimum. But she would have none of it, her nails digging into his buttocks, her own hips lifting from the ground to force him in even deeper. It was too much, Sergio groaning as the last embers of his control exploded into a firestorm of raw passion. When he began pounding into her like some caveman, she came straight away, crying out his name quite loudly. His own climax swiftly followed, his release equally noisy and violent.

They clung to each other like drowning people in a stormy sea, shuddering and shaking, till eventually—after what felt like an eternity—the storm passed. Bella's legs fell limply back to the ground, Sergio levering himself up from where he'd collapsed across her.

Her eyes, when they met his, looked stunned.

'Good God, Sergio,' she choked out. 'That was… That was…'

'Fantastic?' he suggested, using humour to hide his fear that he might be falling in love with Bella. For surely just lust couldn't explain the emotion that had filled him when he'd held her afterwards. He'd never wanted the moment to end.

She laughed. 'That's one way of putting it, I suppose.'

'It's the only way, sweetheart.'

'Please don't call me that,' she said sharply.

'What? Sweetheart?'

'Yes. I'm not your sweetheart.'

God, but that hurt. Oh, yes, he was falling for her all right. Damn and blast. Bella was the last woman on earth he wanted to fall in love with. The irony of the situation did not elude Sergio. His father had fallen hard for her gold-digging mother, and now he was doing the same with the daughter, who could be just as bad, for all he knew. Sergio cursed himself for being stupid enough to confess he was a billionaire. But it was too late now. The damage had been done.

'What would you like me to call you, then?' he asked offhandedly whilst calling himself all sorts of names.

'Just Bella will do fine. I'm your friend with benefits, remember, not your girlfriend.'

'True. And might I say I've never had better benefits.'

Yes, this was the way to play it. Cool and casual. No way would he ever let her know his true feelings. Hell no!

Bella couldn't understand why she was feeling so put out by Sergio's attitude. He was only telling the truth, after all. It worried her that perhaps she was trying to put a romantic spin on her feelings for Sergio. Her mother had brought her up to believe nice girls only went to bed with men they loved. Which is why Bella had had only three lovers in over ten years. Of course, that had been long before her mother had confessed the truth about her marriage to Sergio's father.

It was hard, though, to abandon such long-held beliefs. For a while there just now, Bella had started thinking there had to be something more between them than just sex. It seemed perverse that she'd experienced more pleasure with Sergio than she had with any of her so-called lovers. Perverse also that she should feel so bereft when he withdrew and rolled away from her. In the past, she'd always been relieved when her lover had been finished with her.

'Is sex always this good for you, Sergio?' she asked as he reached for his clothes.

Sergio wanted to weep. Instead, he somehow found a suitably nonchalant voice. 'Not always.'

'I've never felt anything like what just happened,' she said.

Against all common sense, her admission thrilled him. But he dared not look at her, lest she see the light of love glistening in his eyes.

'There's no rhyme or reason to sexual chemistry, Bella,' he lied as he drew on his shorts and T-shirt. 'Sometimes it is better than others. I also suspect you haven't been with a man for quite some time—is that right?' he asked, finally glancing her way.

She was still disturbingly naked and made no attempt to cover herself.

'I broke up with Andrei over a year ago.'

He already knew that, the news having made his day at the time.

'And there's been no one since?'

'No.'

'No one-night stands?'

'I don't have one-night stands.'

'What? *Never?*'

'No, never. I can't think of anything worse than having sex with a virtual stranger.'

'That's very…um…'

'Old-fashioned of me?' she said.

'I was thinking more along the line of unusual in this day and age.'

'I suppose you have one-night stands all the time.'

'Not very often. But there have been times in my life when some mindless sex with a virtual stranger fits the bill.' Like when I was going crazy after seeing you with that French sleazebag. 'Look, if you don't mind, do you think you could put your clothes back on? Unless, of course, you want seconds.'

Bella just stared at him. 'I'm not sure I could manage seconds. I feel a bit wrecked.'

'You don't look wrecked. You look beautiful.'

She flushed. 'I think you're a devil with the ladies too,'

she said, reaching for her clothes. 'Just like your friend Jeremy.'

Sergio shrugged, thinking he was nothing like Jeremy. Jeremy didn't fall in love. He always said falling in love was for fools.

Not that falling in love with a woman as unique and beautiful as Bella should make any man feel a fool. If truth be told, if he put aside his prejudices over whose daughter she was, Sergio could see Bella wasn't a chip off the old block. If she'd been a ruthless gold-digger like her mother, she'd have already married one of her wealthy lovers. That Russian billionaire had been mega rich. Neither was she as promiscuous as he'd imagined. She was actually very sweet and sensitive, a woman worth loving. A woman worth marrying, even.

This last thought shocked Sergio to the core. It was one thing to fall in love with Bella. Another thing entirely to want to marry her. Now that *was* foolish. Aside from the fact that she didn't love him back, Bella didn't want to marry. She'd said so.

But was she telling the absolute truth? Sergio wondered as he started packing up the picnic basket. Maybe she just said that because no man had ever asked her. Maybe it was her pride talking. Sergio hoped so. Because now that he'd had time to accept the truth of his feelings, he realised that falling in love with Bella was a game changer. He would have been content with a month of her in his bed when he'd believed it was just lust he felt for her. But a mere month of sex was no longer on his wish list. He wanted a lifetime of loving Bella, wanted her as his wife and the mother of his children.

Hell, Sergio, you don't make things easy for yourself, do you?

Still, he'd already won over her body. Now all he had to do was win over her heart.

Easier said than done.

'So in your bachelor world, Sergio,' Bella remarked thoughtfully as she dressed, 'does a friend with benefits have to share?'

Sergio wasn't sure what she was getting at. Till the penny dropped.

'I suppose you're referring to the Countess,' he said.

'Call me old-fashioned—or unusual, if you prefer—but I wouldn't like you to go from her bed to mine tonight.'

Sergio liked her being jealous, or possessive. Or whatever you would call it. It wasn't the same as love, but it was a good start.

'I would never go from Claudia's bed to yours, sweet Bella,' he said, and leant over to kiss her lightly on the mouth.

When his head lifted he noted a wealth of doubt still in her eyes. Sergio supposed he had no one to blame but himself. He'd painted himself as a swinging bachelor and was now living with the consequences. He imagined that Bella wasn't about to fall for him—let alone marry him—till he showed he was a man of his word whom she could trust.

'I have never slept with the Countess,' he told her. 'She is a friend and neighbour, nothing more. Look, why don't you come with me tonight? I can easily ring Claudia and explain I have a guest.'

She frowned, then shook her head. 'No, no, please don't. I really don't want to have to wear that silly wig and be introduced as someone else.'

'Then come as yourself. The Countess loves nothing better than to entertain a celebrity in her home.'

'But I thought you wanted to keep my identity a secret!'

'That was before. I realise now that I was being paranoid about the paparazzi. Besides, Claudia won't tell anyone if I ask her not to. On top of that, what kind of holiday is it if you can't relax and just be yourself?'

Her frown dissolved into the loveliest of smiles. 'You really are a very nice man,' she said. 'When you're not being wicked,' she added before he could take her compliment to heart.

'I'm only wicked around you,' he said, and she laughed.

She was still smiling when they boarded the boat.

'What's so funny?' he asked.

'I was thinking how much I enjoy being your friend with benefits. I'm going to miss you when I have to go back to New York.' She sighed. 'If only you didn't live so far away...'

'There are planes, you know, Bella. I can be in New York in a few hours.'

She looked genuinely surprised. 'You'd come and visit me?'

'I think I could be persuaded,' he said, having resolved not to rush things.

'What would I have to do to persuade you?' she asked.

He smiled what he hoped was a devilishly charming smile. 'I'll show you later tonight.'

CHAPTER EIGHTEEN

BELLA WASN'T OFTEN nervous these days. But she felt nervous tonight. Or was it excitement that was making her heart pound as she walked, hand in hand, with Sergio to the villa next door?

I'll show you later tonight...

She hadn't been able to get his erotically charged promise out of her head.

He *was* a devil with the ladies, she accepted. A very handsome devil. He looked utterly gorgeous tonight dressed in tailored black trousers and a snow-white silk shirt, opened at the neck. He'd shaved off the macho stubble he'd been sporting since she arrived, but it didn't make him any less attractive to her. She found his well-groomed appearance even sexier, because she knew the conservative image he projected tonight wasn't the real Sergio. The real Sergio was nothing like she'd always imagined. There was nothing conservative about the man who'd suggested their *friends with benefits* relationship. A shiver ran down her spine as she wondered what more benefits lay in store for her later tonight.

'Are you cold?' he asked straight away.

'A little,' she lied. How could she possibly be cold when her whole body was burning with desire?

'You should have brought a wrap,' he said. 'That outfit you've got on is lovely but not exactly designed to be worn outside on a cool evening.'

Bella was wearing a white pantsuit with flared trousers and a halter-necked top with a mostly bare back. The top was lined but the amount of skin exposed meant that a bra was out of the question. She hadn't brought many clothes with her, but this outfit was a staple with her when travelling. It could be rolled up into a ball then unravelled without a single crease. She'd paid a small fortune for it but her stylist at the time had said the outlay would be well worth it in the end.

And it had been.

It was also a sexy garment that suited her colouring and made her look very tall and elegant when she wore it with high heels. Tonight, however, she'd teamed it with low-heeled silver sandals for the ten-minute walk Sergio had said it would take to reach the Countess's villa. Her hair was up so that it wouldn't be messed up by the breeze from the lake.

'I didn't bring a wrap with me,' she said. 'I packed in rather a hurry.'

'Then let me keep you warm,' he said, folding an arm around her shoulder and pulling her close.

Bella suppressed a groan as she instantly responded, her nipples peaking like bullets against the silk lining, her lower belly tightening. Never in her life had she been so aware of her body, especially that area between her legs that was already throbbing with need. The thought of sitting at some dinner table for hours making small talk with someone she didn't know was horrendous. She would much rather be back in Sergio's bedroom, letting him show her what she could do to persuade him to visit her in New York.

Whatever it was, she would do it. She would do anything to have Sergio in her bed on a regular basis. She could not imagine life without him in it. He made her feel things that she'd never felt before. When she was with him, she didn't feel a failure. Or a bore. She felt deliciously sexy and fabulously free of all those negative emotions that lovemaking had always produced in her. Maybe one day she would find another man who satisfied her as much as Sergio did but she doubted it. He was a fantastic lover, with a magnificent body just made for sex. On top of that, he was a true friend. He didn't try to con her with lies, or seduce her with flattery. He was honest with her. God, but she liked that. A lot.

'We don't have to stay too late, do we?' she asked.

Sergio's heart turned over at the urgency in her voice. She might not love him, but she wanted him. Wanting someone could be very powerful, as he well knew. But it was not love.

Making Bella fall in love with him would require more than just giving her sex whenever and wherever she wanted it. Whilst he did not agree with the popular male mantra of *treat 'em mean and keep 'em keen*, he did understand that the female sex liked a man to be a challenge. In view of that idea, he vowed not to hurry home tonight. He would make her wait. Make her want him very badly. And if his conscience pricked him at this tactic, if there was an element of vengeance in pushing her frustration to the brink, then so be it. Let her suffer a little the way he'd suffered all these years. Let her know what it was like not to have what you wanted.

Sergio suspected it might be a new experience for Bella.

'I'm sorry, Bella,' he said, 'but I couldn't possibly offend Claudia by leaving early. She was most excited when I told her who I was bringing for dinner. Now don't pout. You'll enjoy her company, I assure you. Not to mention her food and wine. The Countess only serves the very best.'

'I am *not* pouting.'

'Oh, yes, you are. And very prettily too. I'd kiss you into a better mood if Claudia wasn't watching us from the terrace. So be a good girl and smile.'

'Good Lord!' Bella exclaimed once the Countess's home came into better view. 'That's not a villa. That's a palace!'

'Not quite, but it is grand, I admit,' Sergio said as he steered her up the steep path towards the stone steps that would lead them up onto the imposingly large terrace. 'Wait till you see the main reception room,' he added before they were within earshot of their beaming hostess. 'Acres of marble and the most expensive antique furniture money can buy. Of course, the Count was very rich. And very old. He died shortly after their first wedding anniversary. Rumour has it he died with a smile on his face.'

'I can imagine,' Bella whispered as they mounted the steps. 'She's very beautiful.'

'But not as young as she looks,' he whispered back, then said, 'Claudia!' in a normal voice. 'How lovely you look tonight.'

'Why, thank you, Sergio,' she replied in her fake Italian accent. Sergio knew full well that she wasn't Italian born, his father having confided in him that she'd come from Albania, having been born into a dirt-poor family a few years after the war. Sergio never let on that he knew the truth about her background. Everyone was entitled to at least one secret in their life. He certainly had his, vowing that he would never tell Bella how much he'd always wanted her. Such knowledge would not enhance his attractiveness in her eyes.

'And this is the very beautiful Bella,' the Countess said, coming forward to take both of Bella's hands in hers. She was a toucher, was Claudia. And very charming. 'Alberto was very fond of you, my dear. Proud too. He went to London to see you perform, did you know that?'

'No, I didn't,' Bella said, looking discomfited by this information.

'He would be very glad to see you and his son together.' Sergio waited for Bella to deny that they had a relationship, but she didn't. She just smiled, then threw him a look that said *please rescue me.*

He wasn't inclined to do any such thing. He wanted Claudia to think they were an item. But he didn't want the whole world to know. Not just yet.

'We're keeping our relationship a secret for now,' he told their hostess. 'Don't want the paparazzi getting wind of it. So as I told you over the phone, Claudia, not a word about her staying at the lake here with me.'

'I will not breathe a word,' she replied with a conspiratorial smile. 'But you must promise me that I will be the first to know, if and when you plan to announce your engagement.'

Bella looked startled whilst Sergio laughed. 'We're not quite at the engagement stage yet. But if and when we are, you'll be the first to know.'

'Wonderful,' she said, clapping her hands together. 'I love any excuse for a party, as you well know. Now we should go inside and into the dining room before Angela comes storming out in search of us. You know how she is. Italian cooks are such temperamental creatures,' she informed Bella.

After that, the evening went smoothly, which was understandable, given the social skills of their hostess. The Countess had the knack of making her guests feel special, her questions never seeming to pry, even if the end result was that she uncovered all sorts of personal details in the process. Bella finally confessed over dessert that she had been feeling seriously burnt out for some time, and probably needed a longer holiday than a month, at which Sergio jumped in and said it would be no hardship for him if she stayed longer. Claudia smiled a knowing smile at that point whilst Bella astounded him by blushing, which seemed out of character for a woman of her age and experience. But then Sergio recalled what she'd told him earlier today about never having had a one-night stand. He'd found that unusual but rather sweet. He found her blushing sweet, yet sexy at the same time.

God, but he had it bad!

The maid appeared just then, the same girl Claudia always hired when she had a dinner party. Angela refused to wait on tables, claiming she was a cook, not a waitress.

'We'll have coffee in the music room, Gina,' Claudia informed her. 'Shall we?' she added, waving imperiously to Sergio and Bella as she stood up.

They exchanged glances as they both stood up, Sergio taking Bella's arm and steering her in Claudia's wake. To reach the music room they had to walk through the main reception room, which had Bella telling him with her eyes that she was seriously impressed. The music room was just as impressive and almost as large, with several intimate seating arrangements and a grand piano situated very grandly in a semi-circular alcove that had floor-to-ceiling windows and a view of the lake that was truly spectacular during the day and still enchanting at night.

When they were seated—on a brocade-covered sofa and chairs, which were more comfortable than they looked—Bella complimented Claudia on the beauty of the room, then asked her if she played the piano.

'Alas, no,' their hostess replied. 'The Count was the pianist. And a brilliant one at that. I loved listening to him play. Do *you* play the piano, Bella?'

'I do,' she admitted, surprising Sergio. He'd never heard her play during the years he'd lived in the same house as her. They hadn't even had a piano. 'Not all that well, however,' she added. 'In the performing arts school I attended, playing the piano was mandatory. We also had lessons in composition. It helps to play the piano if you want to write songs. Of course, most songwriters nowadays use an electronic keyboard rather than a piano. I keep one in my apartment in New York. It cost me the earth but then it does have a lot of features including auto recording, a must if you don't want to risk losing your work.'

'You actually write songs?' Sergio asked, then kicked himself for sounding surprised.

Her expression was rueful. 'Yes, Sergio, I actually write songs. I wrote the main song for *An Angel in New York*. I've earned almost as much money from writing that song as I have from singing it.'

'What a clever girl you are!' Claudia said. 'Ah, here's Gina. Just put the tray down there, dear. I'll pour. Now, after we've had our coffee, I insist you sing that lovely song you wrote, Bella darling. This room has perfect acoustics. You will sound like an angel. An Angel from New York,' she added with her most persuasive smile.

Bella wasn't just clever but exceptionally talented, Sergio was reminded as he listened to her play the piano and sing at the same time. Her voice was as unique as she was. Clear as a bell, with perfect diction, it could soften then soar with effortless ease. But it was the emotion she put into her performances that lifted her talent to a level that had made her the darling of Broadway. She might be burnt out at the moment, but you would never know it listening to her tonight. Singing and performing were her life-blood. Sergio could see that. She could never give it up. Any man who expected her to would be a fool.

Sergio didn't consider himself a fool. If and when…no, *when* he married Bella, he would have to be prepared to put his own working life on hold occasionally whilst he supported *her* career. He would have to learn to delegate so that he could be with her in New York, or London, or wherever her career took her.

It wasn't what he was used to doing. He'd been a very hands-on boss in their franchise business. He'd also been looking forward to the challenge of making the family business a success again. His falling in love with Bella, however, was forcing him to change his priorities. Winning her heart was now number one in his life. The family business would have to take a back seat till that happened. Though who knew? Maybe a miracle would happen and he'd find a way to turn things around during the next month. Of course, the only way to do that was to get started. Pronto. Come tomorrow, he would definitely be driving into Milan to see the lie of the land, up close and personally.

But that was tomorrow, his focus right now was on other things, namely getting Bella back home where he could show her his love by making love to her with some more of the passion he'd bottled up for years. He would have to be careful, however, not to tell her that he loved her in the heat of the moment.

Patience, Sergio, he exhorted himself.

Not one of his favourite virtues.

Finally, he was able to get her away from Claudia without appearing to be in a hurry.

It was Bella herself who almost proved to be his undoing, turning to him as soon as they were out of sight.

'I think I'm going to die, Sergio, if you don't kiss me right here and now,' she said, her voice vibrating with an urgency that echoed his own.

'I think we should wait till I get you home,' he said, trying to keep it together.

'No,' she argued, her face flushing as she wound her arms around his neck and pressed up against him. 'No more waiting. I'm done with waiting. Tonight has been nothing but sheer torture.'

Still, he hesitated. But then he slowly lifted his hands to undo the button at the back of her neck. He peeled the top downwards, till she was naked to the waist, pushing her away from him so that he could look at her, taking in her erect nipples and her rapid breathing.

'If I kiss you now,' he said, his voice low and husky with desire, 'I won't stop at kissing. Your lovely clothes will be ruined and the sex won't be as good as it should be.'

'I don't care,' she cried, her voice and her body trembling uncontrollably.

'But I do,' he told her, and bent to scoop her up into his arms. She gasped, then wrapped her arms tightly around his neck.

'You obviously need more than a quickie in the garden. You need me to make love to you till you can't move a single muscle. I will tie you naked to the bedposts and make you come and come till you beg me to leave you alone. That is what you need, isn't it, Bella?' he ground out as he started carrying her along the path at considerable speed.

She didn't say a word. Just groaned, then buried her face into his chest.

CHAPTER NINETEEN

WHEN BELLA WOKE the next morning, she was astonished to find herself back in her own bed. She had definitely been in the master bedroom when she'd finally fallen asleep last night. Sergio must have carried her back to her room at some stage but she had no memory of it. The clothes she'd worn the night before were draped over a chair in the corner, her sandals placed neatly underneath.

Clearly, Sergio didn't want Maria knowing they were sleeping together. No doubt if she knew, Maria would have them married off even quicker than the Countess. Though how he imagined they could keep their relationship a secret for a whole month she had no idea. Maria was a very intuitive woman.

Sighing, Bella rolled over and glanced at the small antique clock that sat on the mantelpiece over the fireplace. Lord, it was past noon! She hadn't slept so soundly in years. Obviously, a satisfying sex life was the answer to that. And it *was* satisfying. Very. After their first rather frantic mating last night—up against the back of his bedroom door, no less!—Sergio had proceeded to make slow love to her in bed for ages, Bella adoring the way he'd looked deep into her eyes as he'd done so. She'd lost count of the number of times she'd come. It was no wonder that in the end she'd fallen into such a deep sleep, one where she'd been blissfully unaware of being carried back to her own room.

A soft knock on her bedroom door had her sitting up abruptly, pulling the sheet up over her bare breasts.

'Sergio?' she said, feeling perversely shy all of a sudden.

'No, no, it is me. Maria. Sergio…he has gone to Milan. He left a couple of hours ago.'

'Oh, yes. He did tell me he was going there today but I forgot. Come in, Maria.'

She opened the door and bustled in, looking uncharacteristically worried. 'I'm sorry to wake you. Sergio said you had a late night. But I must go home soon. My little Antonio, he has a bad cold and Carlo, he is working on the other side of the lake today.'

'Then you should go home straight away, Maria,' Bella said.

Maria frowned. 'But I have to make your bed and clean your bathroom.'

'I am quite capable of making my own bed and cleaning my own bathroom. Now off you go.'

'Are you sure? What about your lunch?'

'Maria, I am sure I can rustle up something. I saw how much food was in the cupboards and fridge. On top of that, it is only a short walk to the closest village where there is an excellent café and bakery. I have stayed here before, you know. A long time ago, but, as the driver told me the other day, Italy does not change much. And please, do not even think of coming back tonight. I will get Sergio to take me out somewhere for dinner when he gets home from work.'

Maria smiled with relief. 'You are very kind. I will go now, then.'

'Yes, please do.'

After Maria hurried off, Bella lay back on the pillow and sighed, having remembered that Sergio planned to go into Milan *every* weekday from now on, not just today. Which was somewhat disappointing. She'd been hoping to have him all to herself for the next month. Still, the family business *was* in dire straits, he'd told her during one of his brief rests from lovemaking last night. It had, in fact, been losing money for several years, his father not proving to be as astute a businessman as his grandfather.

'Of course, the economic climate has changed,' Sergio had explained. 'So have the markets. Where once Morelli leather goods were huge sellers, both overseas and here in Italy, they now can't compete with the cheaper imports from Asia. We don't have any branches in any other countries any more. They just weren't profitable. We now use independent agencies to try to sell our wares overseas. Without much success, I'm afraid.'

Bella recalled he'd looked very concerned.

'Some of the staff have been with the company all their working lives,' he'd continued. 'My father found it impossible to let any of them go, but I will have to do some restructuring or *all* the staff will be out of work. Luckily, I have plenty of money of my own to invest in some much-needed change. But what those changes will be, I have yet to determine. Hopefully, I will get some inspiration tomorrow when I go through the factory and talk to the employees.'

Bella had made all the right noises, saying she had every confidence in him, but in reality she hadn't been concentrating, her focus distracted by the way he'd been caressing her as he'd chatted away. He couldn't seem to keep his hands off her. Not that she was any better. As the night had worn on she'd become addicted to stroking him very intimately, loving the way she could bring him back to erection within minutes of his having climaxed. She'd been doing just that when she'd playfully asked him what she had to do to make sure he'd visit her in New York. He'd just smiled and said she didn't have to do anything special. Just be there when he arrived at her apartment, wearing nothing but perfume.

A smiling Bella had given him her faithful promise, at which point Sergio had stopped talking and started making love to her yet again.

What amazing stamina he had! And what incredible know-how. He knew exactly how to move when he was inside her. And how to move *her*. She'd been amazed at the various positions he'd shown her. She was already looking forward to Sergio coming home tonight. She would wear something sexy for him. Something new. The village she'd spoken of to Maria also had a nice little fashion boutique. Or they used to. Hopefully, it would still be there.

It was. Though with a new owner. It had also gone very up-market, selling high-end accessories along with designer clothes. Fortunately, the new lady owner didn't recognise Bella despite her not wearing the red wig, though she did fuss over her once she realised money was no object. Bella's stylist had drummed into her that buying quality was always worth it in the end, as long as you didn't buy super-trendy things that would go out of fashion the following year. The owner was delighted when Bella invested in a sundress, a cocktail dress, a pair of shorts, two summery tops and a lovely cashmere wrap, Bella determined to have something for every occasion during her stay here with Sergio. Her last purchase was a pair of sensible but very expensive walking shoes, which would cope with the cobblestone paths better than the sandals she was wearing. Keeping them on, she asked the woman to hold her purchases till she'd had some lunch, which of course she was very happy to do.

Fifteen minutes later, Bella was sitting at an outdoor table connected to a nearby café, eating a delicious salad and drinking some sparkling mineral water when a brilliant idea came to her. At least, *she* thought it was brilliant. Excitement raced through her veins at the realisation that this might be the answer to Sergio's prayers. Bella would have called Sergio immediately with her idea, but she didn't have her phone with her, having deposited it in the top drawer of one of her bedside tables. She'd been determined to remain out of touch with the rest of the world for several days at least; hadn't wanted to be confronted by the long line of missed calls that would inevitably be there, along with a whole swag of unread messages. Her mother would be the main culprit, trying to find out where she was and who she was with.

Bella felt a twinge of conscience at this last thought. She supposed it was a bit mean not to let her mother know she was safe and well. And she wasn't a mean person. If truth be told, she was too kind for her own good, sometimes, especially where her mother was concerned. When her career had first taken off, she'd kept her mother on as her manager for much longer than she should have. Bella had known people didn't respond well to Dolores's aggressive, stage-mother manner. She'd been told more than once that she would do better with a professional manager, someone with the experience and the contacts to take Bella's career to the next level. At the time, she'd been getting only minor roles on Broadway, plus the occasional singing gig on television back home in Sydney.

But she hadn't wanted to hurt her mother. She also hadn't had the confidence to take such a step. She'd only been a teenager, after all.

It had been Raoul coming into her life that had precipitated her finally getting out from under her mother's thumb. An international polo player from Argentina, Raoul had pursued her with the kind of persistence Bella would always find very flattering. Even so, it had taken the Argentinian playboy several weeks to seduce Bella away from her mother's stultifying influence and into his bed. Any satisfaction he had initially found in deflowering Bella, however, had gradually turned to dissatisfaction. He hadn't been cruel when he'd broken up with her but he had been blunt.

'You need to get that mother of yours out of your life, Bella, if you want to become a real woman,' he'd told her.

'She is keeping you like a little girl. You need to grow up and take control of your life, and your career. Get yourself professional representation before it's too late.'

So she had, firing her mother and signing with Josh, who was a top New York agent. Dolores, of course, had put on the biggest tantrum, only alleviated when Bella had signed a contract where her mother still received ten per cent of her income, though only for the next ten years. Which possibly explained why her mother was so keen on her doing that movie, Bella realised, with her gravy train running out in just over a year's time.

Not that Bella would ever see her mother go short of money. Neither did she want her to worry unnecessarily. Bella decided to bite the bullet and give the woman a call this afternoon, but not till after she'd rung Sergio. He was her priority at the moment. It gave her a warm fuzzy feeling to think she might be able to help him with his family business. Hopefully, he would agree that her idea had merit.

Excited now, she finished her lunch, then hurried along to the boutique where she collected her parcels, saying a silent thanks that the clothes she'd bought were not heavy items. Nevertheless, by the time she arrived back at the villa Bella was a little puffed, having walked at a solid pace all the way. Racing up the stairs to her bedroom, she dropped the parcels on the floor, retrieved her phone from the drawer, turning it on as she sat down on the side of the bed. Ignoring the ping that informed her of all her missed calls and messages, she took a few calming breaths, then called Sergio.

He didn't answer for several rings, by which time Bella's heart was racing.

'Bella!' he said at last, anxiety in his voice. 'What is it? What's happened?'

'Nothing's happened,' she reassured him. 'Nothing bad, that is. I went into the village to buy a few things and when

I was there, I had this idea I thought might be helpful for the business. I would have rung you then and there but I didn't have my phone with me. Anyway, I got so excited that I practically ran home so that I could call you ASAP. I haven't rung you at a bad time, have I? You sound stressed.'

'If you'd seen our sales figures you'd be stressed too. You're going to have to be a miracle worker, my darling, to turn them around. But I'm all ears.'

Bella was so taken aback by his calling her his darling that she was speechless for a few seconds. Not that he'd meant anything serious by it. But it had thrilled her all the same. Thrilled her to pieces. The possibility that she was falling in love with him worried the life out of her. Not that Sergio wasn't a man worth falling in love with. He was, his concern for his employees very touching. His spirit was generous, not greedy. Caring, not selfish. As Luigi had said, he was a good man.

But if she did fall in love with him, there was no use fantasising that he might fall in love with her in return. That would be too good to be true. It wasn't going to happen. Sergio would never let himself fall in love with the daughter of the woman who'd ruined his father's life. The truth was he fancied her for the reason men always fancied her. Because they found her beautiful and sexy-looking. Love had nothing to do with his feelings for her.

Best you concentrate on just being his friend with benefits, that sensible inner voice warned her. *Because to start hoping for more is the way to a broken heart.*

'Bella?' Sergio prompted. 'Are you still there?'

'Yes, yes. Still here. Just assembling my thoughts.' *And trying to be sensible.*

'Is this idea of yours complicated?'

'Not really. Just hard to put into words.'

'What's the basic thrust of it? Try to use as few words as possible.'

'Well, the bottom line is your products are too cheap.'

'Too *cheap*! Are you mad? We can't compete, price-wise, as it is.'

'Then don't. You're on a losing battle to nothing trying to compete with imports from countries that can make things for a fraction of what you can. You should do what Italy does best, Sergio. Produce stylish, super-quality products for which you can charge a premium. People will pay over and above for true quality. Trust me. I know. I'm one of them.'

Sergio was silent for a long moment before he answered. 'Yes, I see what you're getting at,' he said slowly. 'My God, Bella, I think you're right. We should be putting our prices up, not down. What a clever girl you are!'

'But only if you lift the quality,' Bella pointed out, glad Sergio couldn't see how her heart had squeezed tight at his compliment. 'You might also have to rebrand and advertise extensively. People need to look at your products with new eyes.'

'Sounds good but that'll take a lot of money, Bella. Money and time.'

'Well, you have plenty of both, don't you, Sergio? It's not as though you have anything else to do.'

His laugh struck an odd note to Bella's ears. 'I dare say you're right again,' he said. 'I don't have anything important on my agenda in the near future, other than flying over to New York occasionally to see a certain person.'

'Oh? And who might that be?' she asked playfully. Yes, this was the way to handle things. No point in putting your heart on your sleeve.

'A very beautiful lady with a very brilliant mind.'

Bella couldn't help flushing with pleasure. And feeling exasperated with herself at the same time. 'You don't have to flatter me, Sergio,' she said a bit tartly. 'I'm a sure thing.'

'Now that, my darling Bella, is something you'll never

be. Look, I'd better get off this phone and have a chat with some of the designers. See what they can do about creating a new top-of-the-range line of shoes and handbags. I suspect they'll be quite excited.'

'That's excellent. Before you go, Sergio, could you bring home some samples of your shoes and handbags so that I can have a look at them and compare them with what I buy?' In truth, she was genuinely curious. And very keen to help.

'Will do.'

'What time do you think you might be home?' she asked.

'Not early. I have a lot to do here. Possibly around seven, seven-thirty. *Ciao.*' And he hung up.

The abrupt termination of the call, plus the realisation that it would be hours before she saw him again, left Bella feeling rather deflated, her brilliant idea having backfired on her a little. Clearly, Sergio was fired up by her suggestions and couldn't wait to get to work on them. Making that scale of changes would be a huge project, however, and would mean his working long hours. She would miss him terribly. At the same time, Bella *was* glad that she'd been able to help him. She'd seen how worried he was, not just about the fate of the family company, but the people who worked there.

Her sigh carried resignation to the fact that she wouldn't have as much of Sergio's company as she would have liked. And she wasn't thinking just about sex. She loved talking to him as well. Loved just being with him.

And the reason for that, she told herself firmly, is that you've *definitely* fallen in love with the man.

Bella groaned, any happiness this realisation brought— she much preferred love to lust—tempered by the reality that it was a one-sided love. Sergio *did* like her. And he desired her. Maybe, after today, he even admired her. But that wasn't the same as love.

Frowning, Bella stood up and wandered out onto the balcony, wondering how she could get Sergio to fall in love with her. Despite being a confident girl where her career was concerned, she wasn't at all confident when it came to men, her past relationships having battered her self-esteem in that regard. Also, there was still the problem of whose daughter she was. That could be a huge hurdle in Sergio's mind. It was a dismaying thought.

In the end, Bella decided all she could do was love him to the best of her ability and hope he eventually reciprocated. She dismissed the idea of telling him she loved him. That would make her sound needy and clingy. A long-time bachelor like Sergio would not respond to a woman who was either needy or clingy. No, she would have to be patient.

Patience, however, was not one of her virtues. Neither was not getting what she wanted. Dolores had unfortunately passed along a degree of stubbornness to her daughter, plus a determination to win. Bella had never wanted to win a man before. In the past, it had all been about men trying to win her.

Bella was mulling over lots of various thoughts when her phone rang.

Her groan carried exasperation at the realisation that she hadn't turned it off after talking to Sergio. She knew who it would be. Who else but her mother? Dolores didn't have the patience to wait for someone to ring her back.

Bracing herself, Bella walked back into the bedroom and over to where she'd left the phone on the bedside table. Picking it up, she checked the caller ID then lifted it to her ear.

'Hello, Mum,' she said calmly. No point in getting herself in a twist. After all, she'd already decided earlier to give her mother a call.

'At last she deigns to turn her damned phone on and answer me!' came the snappy retort. 'What on earth have you been thinking, girl? You have responsibilities. And a career. Or you did have one before you disappeared off the face of the earth without telling anyone where you were going. Do you know how many calls I have had complaining that they can't get in touch with you?'

Bella smiled a rueful smile. Lord, but her mother was just so predictable. She wasn't worried about her daughter's physical safety. Just her career.

'Actually no, I don't,' Bella replied with deliberate nonchalance. 'How many?'

'Too many to recount. Just go to your voicemail or your message bank and you'll see for yourself. Josh is desperate to get in touch with you. And so is Charlie. I'm sure it's about the *Angel in New York* movie. I did ask but they wouldn't tell me.'

Thank heavens.

'I'll ring Josh as soon as I get off the phone to you,' Bella offered. She could not deny being curious. Josh was never *desperate*. But if Charlie had been able to get that movie onto the drawing board again, then her manager would be very excited. And so would she. She loved that musical. Singing the song she wrote for it last night had reminded her just how much.

'That's more like it,' Dolores said. 'Go do it right now. But promise you will ring me back straight away and tell me what's going on.'

'Don't you want to know where I am?' Bella couldn't resist asking.

'Humph! No point in asking that when I know you won't tell me.'

'True. But I still expect you to ask.'

'Do you know you've grown into a very frustrating woman?'

'Takes one to know one, Mum. But at least you called me a woman this time, instead of a girl.'

A heavy sigh wafted down the line. 'I don't want to argue with you, Isabel,' she said, always resorting to her daughter's full name when she was severely irritated.

Bella relented with the teasing. 'I don't want to either, Mum.'

'Good. Then get off this phone and ring Josh!'

Bella did as she was told for once and rang Josh, who informed her that he and Charlie had got together and decided to produce *An Angel in New York* independently with their own money, provided she starred in it. Naturally, she told him she would, but she also stood her ground and said she needed a holiday first. Thankfully, he didn't argue with her, though he did make her promise to be back in New York by the first of August to help them with the casting and the costumes. She agreed, knowing that she couldn't hide away here with Sergio for ever. Her dream holiday had to come to an end some time.

She hung up, feeling an odd mixture of excitement and apprehension. Part of her wanted to tell Sergio about the movie—she was thrilled that it was going ahead—but instinct warned her not to. She'd just made an important connection with him with her ideas for his family company and she didn't want to spoil that by talking about her own career. In the short time she had left, Bella wanted to concentrate on him and his needs. It crossed her mind as she planned out the rest of her day that Sergio was as lonely as she was. He needed her as much as she needed him.

Hopefully, by the time she had to leave Lake Como for the flight back to New York, he would realise that. Hopefully, he would come after her the way he'd said he would. And even more hopefully, he would eventually fall in love with her.

'And who's being the cockeyed optimist now, Bella?' she said to herself as she took a deep breath, then resignedly rang her mother back.

CHAPTER TWENTY

SERGIO RESISTED THE urge to speed on the drive home from Milan to Lake Como, despite his impatience to be with Bella. Not for sex. Sex was not his priority this evening. That could come later. First, he wanted to sit down with Bella over a meal and tell her everything that had happened at work once he'd started putting her truly brilliant idea into action. He'd sent her a brief text just before leaving the office, giving her his approximate time of arrival. But he doubted now that he'd make it by seven-thirty. The traffic was appalling. He'd stop and text her again, but that would only take precious time. A quick glance at his watch brought a sigh of relief. So did the turn-off to Lake Como. He wasn't going to be too late, after all. Maybe just a few minutes…

At seven twenty-five Bella started looking out for Sergio, leaving the back doors open so that she would hear the crunch of his tyres on the driveway. By seven thirty-seven she started to worry. Italian drivers were a little on the hair-raising side, she knew. She toyed with the idea of sending him a text but decided against it. Too clingy and way too needy. But she couldn't help pacing around the kitchen before unnecessarily stirring the Bolognese sauce one more time, her anxiety level rising with each passing minute. Just when she was about to explode with escalating tension, she heard the wonderful sounds of his car arriving.

With great difficulty she stopped herself from dashing outside and throwing herself into Sergio's arms like a loving wife greeting her soldier husband home from a dangerous war.

'Play it cool,' she muttered under her breath as she forced herself to stay put in the kitchen.

Which she did, till he walked in with his arms full of shoe boxes and large plastic bags, his dark eyes glittering with happiness.

'I was getting worried,' she said before she could stop herself.

'I would have texted you but that would have made me even later. Wow, something smells good,' he added, dumping all his parcels on the large kitchen table and coming over to have a sniff of the very aromatic spaghetti sauce, which had been simmering for several hours. 'Yours, or Maria's?' he asked as he lifted his head to smile at her.

'All mine,' she said. 'One of Maria's children has a cold so I sent her home.'

'You're a good woman,' he said, turning to draw her into his arms. 'And a brilliant one. That idea of yours was sheer genius. So a thank-you kiss is definitely in order.'

Without waiting for her to reply Sergio kissed her. Hard. His mouth devouring hers for a delicious length of time, Bella quite breathless by the time his head lifted.

'You are like one of Roberto's pizzas,' he growled. 'One slice is never enough. But you are also like fine wine, my darling Bella. Even better if left uncorked for a while.'

She laughed, loving the way he kept calling her darling. 'Thank you very much. I think…'

'Speaking of fine wine, I recall Jeremy sent me a case of truly wonderful reds last Christmas. I'll just pop down to the cellar and get us a couple of bottles to have with that incredible food you've made us.'

'I still have to cook the spaghetti. Or would you prefer another form of pasta?'

'Spaghetti will do fine. And there's no rush. It will be

nice to sit here with you and talk till it's ready. I have so much to tell you. And show you.'

'Yes, so I see,' she said, nodding towards his mountain of parcels.

He shrugged. 'Wasn't sure which ones to bring. After all, I know next to nothing about female fashion accessories. Like I said, I like my women naked,' he added with a devilish grin. 'Back in a sec.'

She shook her head at him as he left. He really was a bit naughty. But extremely lovable. And very sexy. She was going to find it hard to keep her hands off him till he'd talked himself out. Still, Bella could not deny that she was curious over what his new plans were for the business. She was keen too to have a look at the various samples he'd brought home.

By the time Sergio returned with the two bottles of red, the spaghetti was on and Bella was looking at the shoes and handbags on the table.

'Well, what do you think?' he asked her as he opened both bottles.

'I'm no expert,' Bella said thoughtfully, 'but they all look very good quality to me. Not cheap at all. The leather is lovely and soft on the shoes. And the handbags have timeless classical lines. They're also not too big or too small. Same with the handles. Possibly you could improve the quality of the linings. The material is a bit thin. And the colour is not the best. Black linings are really annoying. I can never find anything in handbags with black linings.'

Sergio nodded. 'I would never have thought of that.'

'Why would you? You're not a woman. Thank heavens,' she added with a saucy look.

He laughed, then poured them both a glass of wine. 'Now tell me what you think of this wine.' And he handed her a glass.

'Once again, I'm no expert,' she said as she swirled the glass, sniffed the bouquet, then took a small swallow.

'Yes, I can see that,' he said with a dry laugh.

'Come now, Sergio, a modern western woman is not going to reach the age of thirty without absorbing a little wine know-how. I can't say red wine is my favourite tipple but this is exceptional. Goes down like silk.'

'Jeremy only drinks the very best.'

'Sounds like a bit of a snob.'

'Oh, he is. But a nice one. You'll know what I mean when you meet him.'

'I can't see that happening any time soon.'

They ate out on the terrace where Bella had already set the table complete with candles. By the time the food was gone and they started on the second bottle of wine, Bella had the full picture of what Sergio's new plans were for Morelli's shoes and handbags.

After hearing Bella's ideas over the phone, he'd immediately called a meeting of all the managerial staff in those departments, right down to the factory floor, explaining to them that they weren't going to try to compete with the cheap shoes and handbags being made in Asia any more. They were going up-market, lifting their quality and prices. He also wanted to introduce a very exclusive and more colourful designer range of shoes and bags—including luggage—which would have limited production but super-high prices.

The reaction he'd received was generally very positive, with only a few older members of staff clearly unhappy about the changes. Apparently, Sergio took these aside after the meeting and offered them all redundancy packages that were too generous to refuse. One of them was a distant cousin who his father had put in charge of the company after he fell ill.

'I gave him a little extra,' Sergio admitted. 'He'd done

the best he could but was too set in his ways to embrace new ideas.'

'You did the right thing, Sergio,' she reassured him, picking up the bottle of wine and refilling Sergio's glass.

He lifted the glass to his lips and took a deep swallow, his eyes carrying a degree of regret. 'I felt bad to begin with but I really had no alternative. It's a case of sink or swim in this economic climate and Morelli's was sinking. Which reminds me...' Now his eyes brightened, as did Bella's spirits. The last thing she'd wanted when she'd come up with her idea was to cause him trouble. 'I've decided that the new designer range of shoes and bags will need a new brand name. I hope you don't mind but I would like to call it Bella.'

'Mind! Why would I mind? It's got exactly the right ring to it.' She threw him a flirtatious smile. 'I think you might just be as brilliant as I am.'

His smile was wry. 'I have a long way to go to catch up with you, my darling. I'm still amazed by that song you wrote. You know, I've never seen that particular show of yours but I'd love to. Are you planning on another season on Broadway any time soon? Maybe I could see it when I come visit you.'

She almost told him then. About the movie. But she didn't. Which was just as well, as it turned out.

'There's no immediate plans for another season,' she said instead.

'Pity. Not that I need an excuse to visit you, mind.' His eyes glittered with desire as they raked over her. 'Have I told you how sexy you look in that dress?'

'No,' she said, her own desire flaring in an instant.

'What say we leave this mess for Maria to clean up tomorrow and pop off to bed?'

Yes, please, her eyes must have told him.

'Come on.' He put down his wine, stood up and held out his hand.

'Do you think I could sleep with you here the whole night,' she asked breathlessly when he pulled her up the stairs and into the master bedroom.

'If that's what you want,' he replied, turning her to face him.

'It's what I want. But is it what *you* want? Maria will think things when she finds my bed unslept in.'

'Maria already thinks things, Bella. She's an incorrigible romantic, like Claudia.'

'It's a common female trait.'

'I thought you didn't like to talk during sex,' he said as he started on the buttons of her dress.

'I never used to. But I'm different with you. You're my friend as well as my lover.'

'That's sweet, Bella, but could we just concentrate on the lover part tonight? I've done enough talking for today.'

She might have said something more but he stopped with the buttons and kissed her till she didn't want to talk either. When Sergio fell asleep an hour later with his arms tightly around her, Bella's heart was full of love for him, and a small measure of hope. She liked it that Sergio wasn't worried about what Maria thought any more.

That was cause for hope, wasn't it?

CHAPTER TWENTY-ONE

'I THINK THERE is something you should know,' Maria said casually two weeks later as Bella walked into the kitchen after seeing Sergio off. She'd got into the habit of rising to have breakfast with him on weekdays, then walking with him to his car and kissing him goodbye like a good little girlfriend. Though of course she'd rather be his good little wife.

'What's that, Maria?' Bella said a bit blankly, her mind still on Sergio.

'Today. It is Sergio's birthday.'

'What? Oh, dear God, why didn't you tell me this yesterday?'

'I was not here yesterday. It was Sunday. Sergio gave me the day off.'

'Sorry. So he did. But you could still have said something this morning. I didn't hear you wishing him a happy birthday at breakfast.'

'I did not wish to shame you.'

Bella knew Maria meant embarrassed. But Bella felt shamed as well. Because she should have remembered his birthday was due around now. They'd always celebrated it during their summer holiday here. Around three weeks after hers. Sergio was five years older. Which made him thirty-five today.

Bella groaned. 'Now I feel terrible. I should have remembered.'

'It is no big deal. Men, they do not care about birthdays

once they are all grown up. But perhaps you could go buy him something today and I will make him a cake.'

'Oh, would you? That would be lovely. And maybe you could cook him his favourite meal.'

'Can no do. His favourite meal is Roberto's pizzas.'

'Then we will order him a couple of Roberto's pizzas. They deliver, don't they?' She recalled Sergio ordering pizzas the first night she was here.

'*Sì.*'

'Wonderful. And whilst I'm in the village buying him a present, I'll also get some of those decadent pastries he likes. What do you think, Maria?'

'I think you love Sergio very much.'

Bella sighed heavily. 'I do, Maria. I really do. But I'm not sure he loves me back.'

'Oh, pah. Of course he loves you back. Sergio, he has always loved you. Ever since you were children.'

'What?' Bella just stared at Maria. 'What do you mean?'

'What you mean what I mean? It is clear, is it not?'

'Not to me.'

Maria shrugged. 'You are blind, like Sergio. He loves you, and soon he will see that. Then he will ask you to marry him.'

Bella could not have been more astonished. 'You honestly think so?'

Maria looked offended. 'I do not tell lies. Only the truth.'

'Oh, Maria, I do so hope you're right. I think I will die if he doesn't love me back.'

Maria rolled her eyes. 'And they say Italians women are drama queens.'

Bella laughed. 'Oh, you are funny. Now I guess I'd better go get myself showered and dressed. I have work to do.'

By lunchtime a very happy Bella was back from the village with a lovely gift for Sergio, a not-too-mushy birthday card and far too many pastries. But they'd all looked so delicious she simply hadn't been able to choose. She found Maria happily humming in the kitchen, the sponge layered cake already cooked but not yet filled and iced.

'So what present did you buy?' Maria asked her straight away.

'A very expensive cologne.' It was from Paris, of course. And was aptly named Seduction.

'He will like that. Sergio is very fashionable these days.'

'He certainly is.'

'I am about to make some lunch. Would you like some?'

'Yes, please.'

They ate their ham and tomato rolls out by the pool, washed down with freshly squeezed orange juice. The day was dry and hot, growing hotter by the second. Bella was contemplating spending the afternoon in the pool when her attention was grabbed by a water taxi pulling in at the small pier that jutted out next to their boatshed. A man alighted. A tall, elegantly built man wearing fawn cargo shorts, a bright purple polo and wraparound sunglasses. He had collar-length wavy brown hair, which glinted in the sunshine as he walked with long, confident strides towards them, an overnight bag swinging by his right side.

Bella did not recognise him in the slightest.

'Maria, do you know who that man is?'

'Sì. It is the English friend of Sergio. He stay here sometimes. His name is Jeremy. His last name is too long for me to remember.'

'Good Lord. Jeremy!' Bella exclaimed just as the man himself was close enough to hear her.

Once he reached the shade of the terrace he swept off his sunglasses and grinned rakishly at her. 'Good Lord,' he said, a speculative glint in his sparkling blue eyes. 'Bella!'

Bella was not surprised that he recognised her. Her face *was* well known. She also presumed he knew she and Sergio had once been stepbrother and sister. According to Sergio they'd been close friends since their early Oxford days.

'And what are you doing here, might I ask?' Jeremy went on in a voice that made a mockery of his pretty-boy image. It was deep and rich and very masculine. 'Or is that a rude question? Have you and Sergio been conducting a secret affair that he never told me about?'

Bella tried not to blush, but failed.

'Well, well, well,' was all he said before pulling out a chair and turning a warm smile towards Maria. 'Hello, Maria, darling. You're looking well. How's that big Italian brute treating you? I mean Carlo, not the birthday boy. Who is where, might I ask? Don't tell me I've come all this way to surprise him and he's not even home!'

Maria stood up, slightly a-fluster also. Bella could see why Jeremy was such a hit with the ladies. He was a charmer all right. And sinfully good-looking. But not her type at all.

'Sergio, he has gone to work,' Maria said coquettishly as she cleared the table. 'In Milan. But he will be home this evening.'

'Well, thank God for that.'

'Would you like something to eat or drink, Mr Jeremy?' Maria offered. 'I am brewing some real coffee. We also have lots of pastries.'

'Sounds good. I'll eat and drink whatever you put in front of me, Maria. Your food is second to none. And your coffee…' He kissed the tips of his fingers before flourishing them wide in a very flamboyant gesture. 'I would come all this way just for some of your coffee.'

Maria gave Bella a droll look that said, *See? Some people like real coffee.*

Bella sighed, and Maria hurried off, Bella wondering exactly how she was going to explain her presence here at Sergio's villa. In the end, she decided the truth was a good start, telling him about her attending his father's funeral last year where Sergio had given her his phone number and said if she ever needed his help, to ring him.

'I never saw you at his father's funeral,' Jeremy said, sounding perplexed.

'I was in disguise. Wore a dark wig and glasses.'

'I see,' he said, nodding. 'I gather, then, since you're here, that you ran into some kind of trouble.'

'Yes. A couple of weeks ago. I was suffering from a case of severe burnout at the time and desperately needed to get away. I remembered Sergio's offer as well as the wonderful holidays I spent here when our parents were married. So I rang and asked to rent his villa for a holiday.'

'And this was a couple of weeks ago?' Jeremy queried, a frown forming on his high forehead.

'Yes, why?'

'No particular reason. Just wondering why Sergio didn't tell me about it. He's usually not so secretive. But surely he's not making you pay rent to stay here.'

'No, no. Of course not. He said that he couldn't rent the villa to me as he would be here some of the time himself. Instead, he suggested I stay as his guest. I was more than grateful, believe me. Admittedly, he did make me promise not to tell anyone where I was going. He was worried the media might get a hold of where I was and the paparazzi would be hovering over the villa in helicopters to take photos of us together. You know what they're like.'

'Not personally. I don't have your kind of public profile. But Sergio still could have told me. I wouldn't have told anyone.' He gave her a long considering look. 'So how's the holiday going so far?'

'Oh…er…it's been very nice. Very…relaxing.' What else could she say? If Sergio had wanted Jeremy to know about her staying here he would have told him.

'You certainly look relaxed,' Jeremy said, his tone a

little dry. 'Sergio's obviously been looking after you very well.'

Bella knew exactly what he was implying. But no way was she about to admit to anything with Sergio at this stage other than friendship. It would be up to Sergio to tell him, if he wanted to. Though if he was serious about her, if he loved her the way Maria thought he did, then why wouldn't he want to tell his friend?

Jeremy wasn't the only one who was beginning to feel perplexed.

Maria appeared at that moment with a ham and tomato roll for Jeremy and a cup of very strong-looking coffee.

'Thanks heaps, Maria,' he said.

'My pleasure,' Maria cooed.

Bella was watching Jeremy tuck into the food when she decided that she couldn't just sit there, wondering. So she came to a decision and stood up. 'If you'll excuse me, Jeremy, I'm going to go up to my room and give Sergio a call. Let him know that you're here.'

'Good idea. And whilst you're talking to him, tell him to get himself home, pronto, so that we can have a proper birthday party.'

'He might not want to do that, Jeremy. He told me last night that he had some very important meetings organised for today.'

Jeremy rolled his eyes. 'Typical. That man is a workaholic.'

'Yes,' Bella said. 'He is. A bit.' But she liked that about him. Liked his perfectionism. Liked his intelligence and capacity for hard work. Of course, she would have preferred that he stay home with her all day instead of driving to Milan; that he would devote every hour of the evening to making love instead of chatting with her about the various changes he'd put in place during that particular day.

But she was in no position to complain, or insist. She

was just his friend with benefits so far, not even a real girl-friend. She'd been hoping that Sergio would say something about that over the last two weeks. But he hadn't, despite their many deep and meaningful conversations. Their sex life was also better than ever, and even more intimate. A starkly erotic image sprung to mind of her being bound to that four-poster bed yesterday. Naked, of course. In the afternoon, in the daylight, with everything exposed to those dark smouldering eyes of his, every part of her body accessible to his large knowing hands. But she'd felt no shame, only excitement and the most exquisite of tensions, followed by the most incredible releases. At one stage he'd left her there, alone, whilst he'd gone downstairs for a reviving swim, returning with his body all cold and dripping wet, straddling her straight away and presenting himself to her mouth for her to…

'Tell you what, Bella,' Jeremy said, interrupting her runaway train of thought.

'What?' she said, hoping she didn't look as hot as she was suddenly feeling.

'Don't *you* ring him. Leave that up to me.'

'But…but…'

'Trust me when I say there isn't a meeting alive which can't be postponed, or shortened, or abandoned altogether. All you have to know is what to say.'

Bella winced inside. She tried to think of a logical reason why *she* should ring Sergio and not Jeremy, but nothing came to her scrambled mind. On top of that he was already getting his phone out of his pocket. In the end, she had no option but to sit back down and try not to look panic-stricken. Though why she should be panic-stricken, Bella had no idea. There was no real reason for her to worry. But worry wasn't always logical. Sometimes, it was instinctive.

As she watched Jeremy fiddling with his phone—obviously bringing up Sergio's number—a feeling of imminent doom swamped Bella. She could not imagine what would be said between the two friends that would burst her bubble of happiness, but she just knew that something would. All of a sudden she wished that she'd told Sergio over the weekend that she loved him. She almost had, several times, but had always changed her mind.

She hoped that it was not too late.

But Bella had an awful suspicion that it was…

CHAPTER TWENTY-TWO

THE MEETING WITH the designers for the new ranges of shoes and bags had just concluded when Sergio's phone buzzed. He smiled when he glanced at the ID of the caller. Trust Jeremy to remember that it was his birthday. Alex hadn't, but then Alex wasn't into birthdays. Rather like Sergio himself. Jeremy, however, had used all sorts of reasons for them to get together over the years, especially after they left Oxford and went their own ways to a degree, birthdays having constituted the perfect excuse for a reunion. They never exchanged presents or cards, just had dinner somewhere swanky where the bill for the wine and meals could have fed a small country for a week. According to Alex, that was.

Well, there would be no expensive get-togethers this year, with Alex in Sydney and Sergio in Milan. Sad, really. But then Sergio remembered his plan to marry Bella before the year was out. His friends would surely come to his wedding.

Sergio refused to countenance the possibility that Bella might not say yes when he finally confessed his love and proposed. Failure, he'd resolved during the last two weeks, was not an option. He loved her too much for that. And felt sure she loved him in return. It was just a matter of waiting till enough time had passed for her to be confident of *his* love. He'd almost said something over the weekend but decided in the end it was still too soon.

He lifted the phone to his ear and said *'Pronto,'* without thinking, his mind still on Bella.

'Good God!' Jeremy boomed. 'Two weeks back in Italy and he's gone native! If I knew how to say happy birthday in Italian I would. But I don't. So happy birthday, dear friend. Have you heard from Alex yet?'

Sergio laughed. 'Are you kidding me? Alex is hard pushed to remember his own birthday. So the answer to that is a resounding no.'

'I dare say he's down there in the great land of Oz, making more millions and giving most of it away.'

'Probably.' Alex had told them years ago that his goal to become a billionaire was so that he could make a difference to the migrant communities he'd grown up in in the far western suburbs of Sydney where unemployment was high and life pretty tough. He'd been able to get out and live a better life himself because of his near-genius intelligence, but he'd never forgotten his roots. As a philanthropist went, Alex was the real deal. 'I've been expecting an email from him,' Sergio said, 'asking for a donation from our share of the franchise deal.'

'Don't worry. It'll come.'

'True. Now enough about Alex, what have you been up to? Bought an ailing advertising company yet?'

'No. But I have bought an ailing publishing company.'

'That's very impulsive of you, considering you don't know anything about publishing.'

'I'm an impulsive kind of guy. Guess what I'm doing right now?'

'Let's see. Reading a manuscript, perhaps?'

'Very funny. I'll be leaving that up to the editors, especially the new gung-ho one I hired this week to put a bomb up the old ones. No, I'm sitting by a fabulous pool with the most beautiful blonde by my side.'

'That's hardly news, Jeremy. Isn't that how you spend most of your summers?' Up till now, besides giving him a hand with the financial side of the WOW franchise, Jeremy had worked as an investment consultant in the London branch of his family's highly successful merchant bank. His consultancy, however, was mostly done by phone or email. He spent winters on the ski-fields of Europe and summers at the family's country home down in Cornwall, with his latest blonde girlfriend by his side. Jeremy had a preference for blondes.

'True,' he said. 'But I don't always spend them on Lake Como.'

Shock—and something else—had Sergio snapping forward on the chair. If Jeremy meant what he thought he meant, then the beautiful blonde by his side was Bella.

Play it cool, Sergio, he warned himself before panic— and a surge of jealousy—took hold.

'You sneaky devil,' he said in what he hoped was a casual tone. 'You tried to surprise me on my birthday, didn't you?'

'Guilty as charged. But I didn't expect you to be absent without leave. I thought you were going to have some time off before you tried to rescue the family firm. Or so you said the day we sold the franchise.'

'I was. Initially. But that was before I invited Bella to stay.'

'Yes, she told me about that. And about her going to your father's funeral. In disguise, no less.'

Sergio sucked in sharply. Clearly, Jeremy had wormed out quite a few details from Bella already. He was good at that. Hopefully, she hadn't told him that they were sleeping together. Though if *she* hadn't, then Maria undoubtedly would. Maybe not directly, but she'd drop enough hints for someone as intelligent as Jeremy to get the gist of things. Sergio didn't mind Jeremy knowing they were having an intimate relationship, or even that he was in love with Bella. What worried him was his saying things to her before *he* had a chance to, things like his thirty-fifth birthday bringing an end to his bachelor status, not to mention his confessed intentions to marry and have a family. He probably wouldn't—Jeremy was no blabbermouth—but Sergio couldn't take the chance.

'Yes, that's right,' he said. 'She came to the funeral to apologise for the way her mother had treated my father. That's how we came to be in touch again. And yes, you're right, I didn't tell you or Alex for reasons which will become obvious in due time. Anyway, Jeremy, enough about that for now. I have a favour to ask you. Don't say anything, just listen. This is important.'

'Okay...'

'As soon as you can, I want you to say you'd like to go up to your room and freshen up. Then, when you're safely alone in the bathroom, ring me again. There are some things I need to tell you. Now be careful what you say right now, since Bella's listening. Just say something like *get away as quickly as you can, Sergio*. Then hang up and go upstairs. Okay? Fire away.'

'You know what they say about all work and no play, Sergio. Still, I suppose we can manage without your company for another couple of hours, can't we, Bella? Just get away as quickly as you can, okay? *Ciao*.' And he hung up.

The relief which came with Jeremy's hanging up almost overwhelmed Bella. Thank God she was sitting down.

'That man needs to get himself a life,' Jeremy muttered, then swallowed the rest of his coffee. 'It's just as well I flew over or he probably wouldn't even celebrate his birthday.'

'You could be right,' Bella said. 'I didn't even know it *was* his birthday, till Maria told me this morning. But Sergio had already left for work.'

'Then it's up to us to see that he has a good time tonight.

Meanwhile, I think I'll go up to my room and freshen up. I might even have a little siesta. Hell, but it's hot here today.'

'Yes, it certainly is.' She might have a lie-down herself, feeling quite exhausted now that the tension of that phone call had drained away.

Jeremy picked up his holdall and went in search of Maria whilst Bella stayed where she was for a while, getting her thoughts together. She decided that once she reached the privacy of her room, she would give Sergio a call so that they could match whatever story they would tell Jeremy about their relationship. Hopefully, Maria wouldn't say anything telling in the meantime. Standing up, she made her way into the kitchen, which was empty, Maria obviously showing Jeremy up to his room, no doubt the guest room on the other side of the master suite.

Bella frowned at this thought. His sleeping in that room tonight would make it awkward for Bella to share Sergio's bed without feeling inhibited. They weren't the quietest of lovers. Unless, of course, all was confessed, then it would hardly matter. Jeremy was a man of the world. Why should he care if they were having an affair? Not that Bella liked the word 'affair'. Surely their relationship had moved beyond that.

'I need to finish Sergio's birthday cake,' Maria said as she hurried back into the kitchen. 'Bella, there are not enough towels in the other guest room. Men need many towels. Could you take some more up for me? The big white ones. You know where they are.'

'Yes, of course,' Bella agreed.

'After the cake is done I must go. I told Sergio this morning I could not stay all day. I have another cleaning job on Mondays. Could you say happy birthday for me?'

'Yes, of course.'

Bella collected a couple of the luxurious white bath sheets from the cupboard in the laundry and carried them upstairs with her, walking along the corridor past her bedroom door, past the master suite and along to the furthest guest room. When she knocked, however, there was no reply. A second knock got no answer either. Possibly Jeremy was in the shower. Thinking laterally, she went back to her room and made her way across it and out onto the balcony in the hope that Maria had left the French doors open. It seemed likely, given the heat of the day. They were open, and Bella peeped inside to check that the room was empty before she went in. It was. She'd just placed the towels on the foot of the bed when Jeremy's slightly muffled but still-audible voice reached her ears.

'Right, Sergio,' it said. 'I've done what you asked. Now what gives where Bella is concerned?'

The voice was coming from the en-suite bathroom, echoing off the marble walls and carrying through the door. Bella knew she should leave the room immediately. No good ever came from eavesdropping. But she was a woman. A woman in love. Desperately in love. How could she possibly leave after her name was mentioned? She actually moved a little closer to the bathroom door.

'Yes, I see,' Jeremy said after a long silence. 'Awkward that. So she knows nothing about your plans to marry a nice young Italian girl who will adore you and give you the family you want without causing you the slightest trouble.'

Bella clasped her mouth to stop herself from crying out. But, oh, the pain that seized her heart. She'd never realised that a broken heart was literally that. She could actually *feel* her heart breaking. Because Sergio did not love her. Not only that, he'd *lied* to her, claiming he wasn't interested in getting married at the moment. And all the while he'd planned on marrying an Italian girl. A *young* Italian girl, Bella thought bitterly.

'I have to confess you've surprised me, Sergio,' Jeremy went on after another lengthy silence. 'I know you always had the hots for Bella, but I thought you despised her. Still, I understand perfectly that the temptation to seduce the woman was too great to resist. Lust isn't one of the seven deadly sins for nothing. But I would advise you to think carefully about where you go from here. No doubt she's good in bed. *Very* good. It's easy to become sexually obsessed with a beautiful woman who knows all the right moves. Or so I've been told. Obsession of that kind is not something I've ever experienced. Have you considered keeping her as your mistress, perhaps? That might work.'

Bella couldn't bear to listen to another word. Somehow she made it back to her room without throwing herself off the balcony. Not that it was high enough to guarantee death. By the time she threw herself onto her bed, however, her heartache was turning to outrage, and anger. So Sergio had despised her, yet had the hots for her at the same time. What a charming thought! And there she'd been, thinking he'd invited her here because he was kind, and good. Everyone kept telling her what a good man he was. Well, he wasn't. He was an out and out bastard. He'd done nothing since she arrived but use her. Her body *and* her brain. It was to be thanked that she'd never told him she loved him. That would have been the ultimate humiliation. This way she could at least extricate herself from this appalling situation with her pride intact.

Rolling onto her back, Bella stared blankly up at the ceiling and tried to work out how best to handle things. But it was a struggle to think, especially when all she wanted to do was surrender to self-pity and cry her heart out. But where would that get her? Bella had never been a habitual weeper or wringer of hands, another legacy from her hard-as-nails mother. When tears actually dared to fill her eyes, she dashed them away with a furious sweep of her hands, hardening her freshly broken heart at the same time and focusing her thoughts on what she should do.

She had to leave Lake Como, of course. And as soon as possible. She would ring Luigi and organise for him to pick her up first thing in the morning. Thank God she'd kept his business card. And thank God she hadn't said anything to Sergio about the movie offer. This way, she had the perfect excuse to fly to New York ASAP. It was a pity that she couldn't exit the villa before Sergio arrived home but that would be too odd. Facing him, however, knowing what she now knew, seemed an almost insurmountable hurdle. But Bella was used to facing insurmountable hurdles. You didn't get to be a Broadway star without developing a lot of character, not to mention a hide as thick as an elephant.

Bella hoped she was as good an actress as Charlie kept telling her she was, because she was going to need all her acting skills in the coming hours. In a perverse kind of way she would almost enjoy telling Sergio that she had to leave tomorrow. He might not love her but he sure as hell enjoyed making love to her.

Though of course it wasn't making love, was it? It was just sex. Jeremy had accused him of being sexually obsessed with her. Another depressing thought. Still, it wasn't the first time a man had become sexually obsessed with her. In the past, such obsessions had quickly waned, once they'd discovered she was a bore in bed. This time, however, she'd been anything but boring in bed. She'd responded and behaved like the woman of the world Sergio obviously believed she was; the bed partner of many bad-boy lovers who was prepared to do anything and everything in pursuit of physical pleasure.

Maybe he didn't believe she was promiscuous any more—surely he'd gleaned *something* of her true character by now—but the truth was he had thought exactly that in the beginning. But he'd still seduced her, oh, so cleverly, had still had her every which way a man could have a woman, had still tied her to his bed and done things that didn't bear thinking about. And all the while he'd been planning to marry another woman and keep her on the side as, yes…his mistress.

So much for your silly dreams, Bella. So much for love.

Suddenly, she could not wait for Sergio to get home. Couldn't wait to tell him that she was leaving the next day. Couldn't wait to pretend that it was of no concern to her. They were just ships passing in the night. Just friends with benefits. And when he suggested coming over to visit her—and he would, she just knew he would—she would tell him very casually that it would be best if they called it a day.

It's been a lovely interlude, Sergio darling, she could hear herself say. But now I have to get back to my real life. I'm sure you understand.

CHAPTER TWENTY-THREE

SERGIO WASN'T AT all prepared for Bella's announcement later that night that she had to fly to New York the following day. He stared at her with sinking spirits as she explained that she'd accepted the lead role in a movie version of *An Angel in New York*, and had been summoned to the producers' table ASAP. He struggled to find the words to congratulate her, knowing immediately that all his plans to make Bella his wife had just been seriously derailed.

The evening—which so far had been quite good fun—suddenly lost all its lustre.

'Well, that's wonderful!' Jeremy exclaimed with hearty enthusiasm. 'Isn't that wonderful, Sergio?'

It was no use. He simply could not pretend to be happy for her when he wasn't.

'I thought you didn't want to go into the movies,' he said grumpily.

'I never actually said that. And this isn't any old movie. I would never turn down an opportunity to make *An Angel in New York*.'

'Fair enough. But why do you have to rush off like this? Surely you can stay another week or two. Tell the powers that be that you're still suffering from a serious case of burnout and need some more time off.'

'But that would be a lie, Sergio darling. The last couple of weeks I've spent here have worked wonders. I'm sleeping like a log every night and have more energy than I know what to do with, so I have no legitimate excuse not to get back to work. Trust me when I say when an excellent opportunity like this comes along, you don't make waves. If a top agent like Josh says jump, you say how high.'

Sergio just stared at her, unable to find the right words. Never in his life had he experienced such confusion. He'd always known what to say when things got tricky, or sticky. Always had a clear head under pressure.

Bella's imminent departure, however, had thrown him for six.

'I've booked Luigi to pick me up very early in the morning,' she went on. 'My flight goes around nine so I have to be on the road by six.'

'You didn't have to do that,' Sergio said more sharply than he'd intended. 'I would have driven you to the airport.'

'That's sweet of you, Sergio, but I thought you might like to spend some extra time with Jeremy, since he's gone to the trouble of coming all this way. No, I think it's best that I go with Luigi, but thank you for the offer.'

Her smile, he thought, was oddly false, pricking a memory of a feeling he'd had when he'd first arrived home and she'd been overly vivacious with him. He'd wondered at the time if it was because of Jeremy's presence, the way she'd thrown her arms around him and kissed him before wishing him a happy birthday and apologising profusely for having forgotten.

'Thank God for Maria telling me this morning,' she'd fairly gushed. 'It gave me the opportunity to buy you a present.' Which she'd pressed upon him, smiling when he'd opened it and seen that the cologne she'd bought him was called Seduction. 'An appropriate name, don't you think?' she'd added flirtatiously.

Sergio recalled being taken aback at the time, because it wasn't like Bella to be either gushy or overly flirtatious.

Neither was it like her eyes to go cold when she looked at him. As they were doing now.

Something was wrong. He could *feel* it.

'If you'll excuse me, I must go and pack,' she said before he could work out what was going on. 'Then I might turn in. I'm sure you two boys have lots to talk about, and some more of that fabulous wine to drink. So I'll love you and leave you. I dare say I might not see you in the morning, Sergio, so I'll say my goodbyes now.' He struggled not to shrink back when she came over to give him a very platonic peck on the cheek.

'You've been a wonderful host,' she continued as he just stared up at her. 'I haven't had a holiday this relaxing in years. I'll send you a text once I'm in New York, let you know I arrived safe and sound. Lovely to have met you, Jeremy,' she tossed off as she headed for the doorway. *'Ciao.'*

She was gone before Sergio could jump up and stop her. Though what he could possibly say at that juncture he had no idea. He was totally flummoxed by Bella's total change of character. This wasn't the warm, wonderful woman he'd come to know and love. None of this was making any sense to him.

He whirled towards Jeremy, who was sitting with legs outstretched at the kitchen table, a glass of red in one hand and a half-eaten slice of pizza in the other.

'What in hell did you say to Bella after I rang you?' Sergio demanded angrily.

'Absolutely nothing,' Jeremy said, indignation in his voice. 'I didn't even see her again till you came home. After we spoke, I had a shower, then lay down and fell asleep. For pity's sake, Sergio, what kind of blithering idiot do you take me for?'

Sergio's shoulders sagged as he slumped back in his chair. He still could not believe that she was leaving him like this; that she was leaving him at all! He'd been so sure this last weekend that she loved him, convinced that only a woman in love would trust him with her body the way she'd trusted him. He'd almost told her he loved her a dozen times. He wished now that he had. Because then he would at least know the truth. As it was, he was now left floundering with a whole host of conflicting thoughts and emotions.

'If you want my honest opinion,' Jeremy said, 'then I think her leaving could be all for the best. It's perfectly obvious that she doesn't have the same intense feelings for you that you have for her. If she did, she wouldn't be bolting off back to New York like this. Bella's one priority in life is her work. That's why she's never married. Because she's married to her career.'

Sergio winced at Jeremy's brutally honest assessment. There had to be some truth in what he said. Bella had never married, yet surely at least one of her past lovers would have proposed. At the same time, he still could not accept this sudden decision of hers to leave tomorrow, some inner instinct telling him that something was very wrong.

'You could be right,' Sergio ground out, 'but I'm not going to let her go without telling her how I feel about her.'

'Not a good idea,' Jeremy warned when Sergio stood up.

'Possibly not,' Sergio bit out. 'But it has to be done.'

Jeremy sighed. 'Be it on your head, then.'

Bella was slowly packing and trying not to cry when the inevitable knock came on the bedroom door. She'd known he would come; known he wouldn't let her get away as easily as that. Frankly, she'd been bargaining on it.

Taking a deep breath, she walked over to the door and only half opened it, standing there so that he couldn't come into the room itself. The sight of the obvious distress in his eyes almost undid her determination to be as ruthless as he had been. She'd expected him to be upset with her. Just not *this* upset. Till she reminded herself that he was obsessively in lust with her. Of course he wouldn't want to let her go just yet. He obviously hadn't had enough.

Maybe after yesterday he'd been planning on even more kinky fun and games.

This was exactly the train of thought she needed to steel her spine and harden her heart.

'Yes, Sergio?' she asked crisply. 'What is it?'

His dark brows drew together in a frustrated frown.

'What *is* it?' he threw at her, his head shaking from side to side in seeming disbelief. 'You ask me that after what we've shared this last couple of weeks? I thought what we had was special, Bella. Clearly, I was wrong,' he snapped.

She found a smile from somewhere. 'Oh, no, Sergio, you were quite right. What we shared was very special and I will be eternally grateful to you. If it wasn't for you, I'd foolishly keep believing that I could only enjoy sex with the sort of man I even more foolishly keep falling in love with. Now I know that all I need is a gorgeous-looking male friend like you. Admittedly, I doubt I'll find too many male friends in future who are built as impressively as you are, darling, but that's the way it goes. Look, I know I said I wanted you to come visit me in New York once in a while,' she rattled on, 'but I honestly think we should leave things as they are…'

The icy coldness in his eyes sent tiny shards of glass stabbing into her already broken heart.

'I see,' he bit out. 'There's no more to be said, then. Goodbye, Bella. Good luck with the movie.'

And he was gone, striding off down the corridor without a backward glance. With a strangled sob, she closed the door, then put her head in her hands and wept.

CHAPTER TWENTY-FOUR

'OH!' MARIA EXCLAIMED when she walked into the kitchen just after seven the following morning. 'You are already up. And dressed.'

Her eyes narrowed at this last remark, noting perhaps that her boss looked as if he'd slept in his clothes. Which he had. After that last soul-destroying encounter with Bella, he'd returned downstairs where he'd polished off two more bottles of wine all by himself, at which point Jeremy had told him he'd had enough, then helped him up to bed. He'd woken when he'd heard Luigi's car on the gravel around six, not rising till Bella was safely gone, at which point he'd come downstairs where he'd proceeded to have two mugs of strong coffee in a vain attempt to make a dent in his hangover. He was now on his third.

Maria's frown deepened. 'Something is wrong,' she said. 'Where is Bella?'

'Gone,' Sergio growled, then gulped down some more coffee. He didn't want to talk about Bella. Or even think about her. He should have known what she'd be like all along. She was Dolores's daughter, after all.

'Gone where?' Maria persisted.

'Back to New York. To make a stupid movie.'

'But...but she is coming back, is she not?'

'No, she is not!' he snapped.

'But she *loves* you,' Maria exclaimed, sounding truly horrified. 'And you love her.'

Sergio laughed. 'Well, you got that half right, Maria. I

do love her. At least I did. But she doesn't love me back. She told me so.'

'Oh, pah, that is rubbish! She told *me* she love you very much. But like you, she is not sure you love her. She said she die if you don't. She want to marry you. Be your wife. Have your *bambinos*.'

Sergio's heart flipped right over. 'She honestly said that? That she loved me and wanted to marry me?'

Maria's hands found her hips as they did whenever she was exasperated. 'I do not tell lies! So what happened to make her leave? What stupid thing have you said now?'

Sergio struggled to think. 'I don't know. I honestly don't know.'

'Everything was good yesterday. Maybe Mr Jeremy said something when she took him up the towels.'

'What? When was that?'

'Just before I go. He went upstairs to shower and I worry he might not have enough towels. I ask Bella to take him some more.'

'You sent her up to Jeremy's room with some towels?' Sergio said, his mind racing as he tried to picture what might have happened.

'*Sì*. Are you deaf now as well as stupid?'

Sergio jumped up from his chair. 'That's it. That has to be it!' Excited and appalled at the same time, he raced upstairs and burst into Jeremy's room without knocking.

'Wake up, Jeremy! Wake up!'

Jeremy bolted upright in the bed with a startled gasp. 'What the…? What's going on?'

'Go into the bathroom, close the door, then say something to me.'

'Huh?'

'Just *do* it!'

Jeremy staggered, naked, into the bathroom and closed the door. Sergio groaned when he heard his friend's deep voice as clear as a bell. Without taking the time to explain, he ran to his room, grabbed a fresh shirt and his phone, then bolted for the garage. He was on the road to Milan within five minutes, his heart in his mouth but hope in his heart.

Bella was sitting in a quiet area of the first-class lounge, staring blankly through the large plate-glass window at the comings and goings of the airport, when a pair of black trousers materialised in the corner of her eye. She groaned silently at the thought some man was going to try to pick her up. It had happened before when she'd been waiting for a flight in first-class lounges.

'May I join you?' a very familiar voice asked.

Shock had Bella's head jerking round and up, the silky hair of her red wig swinging around her ears.

'Sergio,' she choked out, thinking how dreadful he looked, his beautiful brown eyes all bleary and blood-shot. 'What…what are you doing here?'

He sat down in the chair opposite her, his expression an odd combination of resolve and remorse.

'I have come to tell you that I *love* you, Bella,' he said in a heartfelt voice. 'And I *know* you love me back. Maria told me so this morning in no uncertain terms. And she does not lie. I also finally worked out what happened yesterday. You took towels up to Jeremy's room and overheard one side of our telephone conversation. You heard him say that I planned to marry a young Italian girl, plus other possibly damning things as well. What you didn't hear, however, was what *I* was saying. I told Jeremy how much I loved you and wanted to marry you. I told him that that stupid plan about marrying an Italian girl had gone out the window within a day of your coming to the villa. He was the one who had doubts. Not me. Never me.'

When Bella absorbed the sincerity in his voice and saw

the love in his eyes, she could not help it. She burst into tears, her shoulders shaking as she sobbed with happiness and relief. Sergio loved her. He hadn't been using her. He *loved* her!

'Please do not cry, my darling,' Sergio choked out as he reached over and took her hands away from her tear-streaked face.

Her seeming distress sent lots of worried eyes swinging their way, one gentleman actually coming over to say something to Sergio in Italian, his voice sharp with disapproval.

Sergio said something back to him and the man smiled, before turning to speak to the other curious patrons. They all smiled then, with one woman actually clapping.

'What did you say to him?' Bella asked after she got her crying under control.

'I told him I'd just proposed to you. And that you were crying with happiness.'

'Oh…'

'So now I had better ask you officially,' he said, winding his fingers through hers. 'Will you do me the honour of being my wife, my darling Bella?'

Bella struggled to swallow the huge lump in her throat. Blinking back a new rush of tears, she bent down to kiss his hands before glancing up at him with still-glistening eyes. But her voice was quite steady when she finally said, 'Yes, my darling Sergio. I will.'

A ragged sigh shuddered from his lungs. 'I am in danger of weeping myself. Which will never do. Let's get out of here.' And he pulled her to her feet.

'But what about my luggage?' Bella asked breathlessly as he hurried her away. 'It's already on the plane.'

'Once I tell them that you won't be on the flight they will unload it. I will get Luigi to pick it up later and take it to the villa.'

Bella just shook her head, in awe of this man she loved. 'What would you have done if you hadn't got here in time? What if my plane had already taken off?'

'I would have caught the next flight to New York,' he replied without missing a beat.

'Really?'

'You'd better believe it. I wasn't about to let you get away, my darling.'

Bella had never felt so loved as she did at that moment.

When they emerged from the terminal several minutes later, Bella was amazed to see Sergio's silver Alfa Romeo waiting for them at the kerbside, a uniformed security guard holding the passenger door open for her.

'Now there is one thing I must ask *you*,' Sergio said once they were safely out of the airport and on their way, not back to Lake Como but heading for the Morelli factory. 'Is there really a movie deal, or did you just make that up?'

'No, it's real all right. But they don't need me in New York till the first of August,' she confessed.

'I see,' he said thoughtfully.

'If you don't want me to do it, Sergio, I won't. I'll give up my career entirely if that's what you want.'

His shock was genuine. 'I would *never* ask that of you, Bella. That wouldn't be right. And it wouldn't work in the long run. You were born to perform.'

Bella bit her bottom lip as a new wave of emotion threatened to overwhelm her. How lucky was she that she had finally found that dream husband she'd always wanted and who she'd imagined did not exist.

'I don't have to work all the time, Sergio,' she reassured him. 'I will want to take lots of time off to be here in Italy with you, especially when the children come along.'

'You do want children, then?' he asked, sounding a little surprised.

'I would *love* to have children. Especially your children.'

'You've no idea how glad I am to hear that. Maria said you did but I thought she might have been getting a little carried away. Oh, dear God…'

'What?'

'I need to ring Maria and Jeremy and tell them everything's sorted out between us. When I found out what had happened, I just bolted out of the place without explaining anything. Here! Take my phone and ring Jeremy. His number's in the menu.'

Sergio couldn't help smiling as he listened to Bella explaining everything to Jeremy. He could well imagine that doubting Thomas choking on the news that they were going to get married.

'And tell him to tell Maria,' Sergio said at one stage. 'Also, we won't be back at the villa for a while. After I do what I have to do at work, I'm taking you ring shopping.'

'Jeremy said congratulations,' Bella informed Sergio once she'd hung up. 'You know, I wasn't sure about him when he first arrived, especially after what you said about him being a Don Juan. But it's hard not to like him, isn't it?'

'Yes. He's very charming. And a very good friend. But he's terribly cynical about love.'

'He might surprise himself and fall in love one day. The way we did.'

'I wouldn't hold your breath.'

Bella nodded. 'I suppose not everyone can be as lucky as us. Sergio, would you mind if I asked you about something I overheard Jeremy say yesterday? Nothing too bad, I assure. Just something which puzzled me at the time. And still does.'

'Ask me whatever you like,' he replied. 'I want no secrets between us.' Except perhaps my rather ruthless intentions when I first invited you to stay.

'Okay… So how long, exactly, have you had the hots for me?'

Sergio chuckled. 'Would you be scandalised if I told you since your sixteenth birthday?'

'Good Lord! *Truthfully?*'

'Cross my heart and hope to die.'

'So when I kissed you and you acted like a dead fish, then you were just pretending?'

'Uh-huh.'

'But I don't understand. Why did you have to pretend like that?'

'You were my stepsister at the time. It wouldn't have been right.'

'I wouldn't have minded.'

'Your mother would have.'

'Oh, dear heaven, my mother! Can you imagine how she's going to react when I tell her we're getting married? She'll probably have a pink fit.'

'She'll cope, once you tell her I'm a billionaire.'

Bella grinned. 'You could be right there.'

Sergio knew he would have to cope with Bella's mother too. But he would. For Bella's sake.

'So you have to be in New York on the first of August,' he mused aloud.

'Yes, I'm afraid so.'

'That gives me two weeks to get things settled at the factory, put someone new in charge and go with you.'

'You're going with me?'

'You don't think I'd let you go to the city of sin by yourself, do you?'

Bella rolled her eyes. 'Sergio, I have lived in New York for years. I know how to look after myself. But I don't mind if you come with me,' she added, blue eyes sparkling. 'Provided you don't go all super possessive and protective like some Italian men do.'

'I'll be as super possessive and protective as I like, Bella. You're going to be my wife.'

Bella sighed. 'Oh, dear…'

'Just kidding. So how long do you think it will take to shoot this movie?'

'Not too long. Two months, perhaps? But we'll have to rehearse for a while first. Get the locations booked and the costumes made. Might take the rest of the year.'

'In that case we'll have to get married before we go. Or is that too fast for you?'

'Not at all. But can a wedding be organised that quickly?'

'We might have to get a special licence. Bribe an official or two. But that shouldn't prove too difficult. This is Italy,' he replied, with a twinkle in his eye.

Bella took a deep breath. 'There is one thing I should confess, since we're not going to keep any secrets from each other.'

Sergio stopped breathing for a second. Please, God, not anything too bad, he prayed.

'I know you're going to have a hard time believing this,' she went on, 'but you are the only man who has ever satisfied me sexually. Before you I was boring in bed. Boring and shy and a total failure. My lack of passion—for want of a better word—was what broke up most of my relationships. But I was none of those things with you. Right from the start, Sergio. Right from the first moment I looked down at you from the balcony and saw you by the pool. Lord, but you took my breath away. You might find this a silly romantic notion but I think Maria was right. I was different with you because you loved me the way those other men never loved me. You are the man I've been waiting for all my life. My dream man. My wonderful Sergio…'

Sergio found himself totally blown away with her confession. She made him feel ten feet tall. And very loved.

'And I have been waiting for you all my life, my darling Bella. My darling Izzie…'

Sergio's heart turned over at the thought of how close he had come to losing her. So very close.

He vowed right then and there that he would do everything in his power to be the very best husband he could be so that she would never regret trusting him with her love. Fancy her offering to give up her career for him. How wonderful was that? But then she was wonderful. And she was all his. He aimed to keep it that way, till death did them part.

* * * * *

#3421 A DIAMOND DEAL WITH THE GREEK
by Maya Blake
Arabella "Rebel" Daniels would rather skydive naked than agree to Draco Angelis's outrageous suggestion. But, unbeknownst to Rebel, her father embezzled money from the formidable magnate, and now *she* must pay back the debt by whatever method Draco demands!

#3422 INHERITED BY FERRANTI
by Kate Hewitt
It's been seven years since Sierra Rocci left Marco Ferranti on the eve of their convenient wedding. But now that she's back in Sicily, Marco needs Sierra's help with his latest business venture and is determined to claim their wedding night!

#3423 ONE NIGHT TO WEDDING VOWS
by Kim Lawrence
Lara Gray is consumed by the passion awakened within her after one night with Raoul Di Vittorio. But what she doesn't know is that Raoul needs a temporary wife, and he thinks Lara is the ideal woman for the job!

#3424 THE SECRET TO MARRYING MARCHESI
Secret Heirs of Billionaires
by Amanda Cinelli
Read all about Italian billionaire Rigo Marchesi's secret love child with London actress Nicole Duvalle. This bombshell could destroy CEO Rigo's latest business deal. Unless the rumors that the baby scandal will have a fairy-tale ending are true?

YOU CAN FIND MORE INFORMATION ON UPCOMING HARLEQUIN® TITLES, FREE EXCERPTS AND MORE AT WWW.HARLEQUIN.COM.

HPCNM0316RB

REQUEST YOUR
FREE BOOKS!

✦**HARLEQUIN**

Presents

2 FREE NOVELS PLUS
2 FREE GIFTS!

PASSION
GUARANTEED
SEDUCTION

YES! Please send me 2 FREE Harlequin Presents® novels and my 2 FREE gifts (gifts are worth about $10). After receiving them, if I don't wish to receive any more books, I can return the shipping statement marked "cancel." If I don't cancel, I will receive 6 brand-new novels every month and be billed just $4.30 per book in the U.S. or $5.24 per book in Canada. That's a saving of at least 13% off the cover price! It's quite a bargain! Shipping and handling is just 50¢ per book in the U.S. and 75¢ per book in Canada.* I understand that accepting the 2 free books and gifts places me under no obligation to buy anything. I can always return a shipment and cancel at any time. Even if I never buy another book, the two free books and gifts are mine to keep forever.

106/306 HDN GHRP

Name _____ (PLEASE PRINT)

Address _____ Apt. #

City _____ State/Prov. _____ Zip/Postal Code

Signature (if under 18, a parent or guardian must sign)

Mail to the **Reader Service:**
IN U.S.A.: P.O. Box 1867, Buffalo, NY 14240-1867
IN CANADA: P.O. Box 609, Fort Erie, Ontario L2A 5X3

**Are you a current subscriber to Harlequin Presents® books
and want to receive the larger-print edition?
Call 1-800-873-8635 or visit www.ReaderService.com.**

* Terms and prices subject to change without notice. Prices do not include applicable taxes. Sales tax applicable in N.Y. Canadian residents will be charged applicable taxes. Offer not valid in Quebec. This offer is limited to one order per household. Not valid for current subscribers to Harlequin Presents books. All orders subject to credit approval. Credit or debit balances in a customer's account(s) may be offset by any other outstanding balance owed by or to the customer. Please allow 4 to 6 weeks for delivery. Offer available while quantities last.

Your Privacy—The Reader Service is committed to protecting your privacy. Our Privacy Policy is available online at www.ReaderService.com or upon request from the Reader Service.

We make a portion of our mailing list available to reputable third parties that offer products we believe may interest you. If you prefer that we not exchange your name with third parties, or if you wish to clarify or modify your communication preferences, please visit us at www.ReaderService.com/consumerschoice or write to us at Reader Service Preference Service, P.O. Box 9062, Buffalo, NY 14240-9062. Include your complete name and address.

HP15